PLANET OF THE APES

RESISTANCE

by John Whitman

Based on the motion picture screenplay
written by William Broyles, Jr., and
Lawrence Konner & Mark Rosenthal

HarperEntertainment
An Imprint of HarperCollins*Publishers*

HarperCollins books are available at special quantity discounts for bulk purchases for sales promotions, premiums, or fund-raising. For information please write: Special Markets Department, HarperCollins Publishers Inc., 10 East 53rd Street, New York, NY 10022.

ISBN 0-06-008374-3

First printing: April 2002

Visit HarperEntertainment on the World Wide Web at www.harpercollins.com

10 9 8 7 6 5 4 3 2 1

CHAPTER ONE

Daena stepped forward and heard a twig snap. In the quiet forest the sound carried like a thunderclap, and she froze, listening. A few feet away, her friend Birn froze, too, and threw her a warning look. On the other side, a boy named Pak suddenly appeared beside her. Pak had a gift for moving through the woods as quietly as a mouse and as quickly as an ape.

"No noise," Pak whispered. "He'll hear."

"I know," Daena snapped back. "Don't lose him."

Pak turned and vanished into the underbrush. Daena turned her eyes forward, searching for movement. Through a line of trees, she spotted what she was looking for. A figure moved along a path a dozen yards ahead, its back to them. Daena crept forward again, careful where she stepped. She slipped past branches, or moved them gently aside the way Pak had done. Birn practiced, too. He seemed to be better at ambush than she was—more patient, more cautious. Daena wanted to charge forward. But a move like that would almost certainly alarm their prey, and that could lead to disaster.

The figure ahead continued along the forest path for another few minutes. Then, with a cautious glance backward, it stepped off to one side and disappeared. Daena and Birn glanced at each other and hurried forward, trying to remain as quiet as possible. The two young humans met on the path at the spot where their target had vanished.

"Do you think he heard us?" Birn whispered.

"I don't know."

"He could have heard us. Apes could have heard us—"

"I don't think he did," Daena insisted. "Maybe this is where he was going anyway."

Pak appeared again. He was shorter than Birn, even shorter than Daena, with wild dark brown hair twisted into thick, uneven braids. But he was built broad and thick, and even though he was just turning from a boy into a man, he already had muscular arms. "The wind is shifting. We're not downwind anymore. He could smell us."

"*He* can't smell us, I'm sure of that," Daena said.

"Maybe, but it's not good practice," Pak said.

"Come on," Daena said. She stepped off the path, following their target's trail.

To her relief, they found him not too far away. A short distance off the main path, the forest growth gave way to a wide, private clearing. There they saw their prey. He had obviously come here often. Tools, piles of wood, and animal skins were strewn about everywhere. Some of them had been assembled into weird shapes. She was surprised that their target had managed to do this kind of work so close to the human camp without being discovered. She would have to tell her mother about it, when this was all done.

The figure in the clearing turned, and all three children dropped low behind a bush. Through an opening in the brush, Daena looked at his face.

He was human, of course. They had pretended he was an ape, with an ape's sense of smell and hearing, because it helped them practice their own skills. But none of them would ever try to hunt a real ape. That would be suicide, especially for teenagers like them.

"What's his name again?" Pak whispered.

"Mad Luc," Daena answered. "He wanders off on his own a lot. Not afraid of the apes. They say it's because he's too smart to get caught."

"They say it's because he's too *crazy*," Birn replied. "He's cracked like a nut. Look at him."

They watched. Mad Luc, an older human in his late forties, was sitting in the middle of the clearing, touching two or three sticks together repeatedly and muttering to himself. The sticks made a *click-click* sound as they touched.

"That's why we picked him to practice our hunting on, remember?" Birn added. "No one was going to care if he complained about us. No one would probably even believe him."

Pak gasped. "Look! Magic!"

Out in the clearing, Luc had just managed to connect the two sticks he was holding. They had formed a cross, and some thin material had been stretched across them like a sheet. The whole contraption was tied to a long piece of string. What had caused Pak to shout was the fact that, as Luc held the thing up, it seemed to rise into the air by itself. "Magic," Pak whispered again.

Daena rolled her eyes. To Pak, everything that he did not understand was magic. Pak was a wilding—he was as human as she was, but from one of the clans that had slowly shed any of the knowledge that humans had gained. The wildings believed that anything apes knew or practiced was evil, so they gave up learning, they abandoned fire, and they lived in the wild like animals. Daena, on the other hand, was a tek—her people did everything they could to preserve their knowledge and make it grow. There were even teks, like her mother, who believed that someday humans could even become as smart as the apes.

"It's not magic," Birn whispered back. "It's . . . it's . . . " but he couldn't explain it at first. The little stick cross with the sheet spread across it was rising into the air. There was a long cord attached to it, and the floating thing was tugging at the string, trying to escape.

"It's the wind," Daena guessed. She felt the breeze on her face, and saw the direction in which the flying thing was tugging. "Somehow it catches the wind."

Pak frowned and cocked his head to one side. "Can this magician make thunder, too?"

"Thunder?" Daena asked. "What do you—?"

"Get down!" Pak said. He grabbed the other two teens and dragged them down into the brush.

At that moment, a band of riders charged into the clearing. Daena stifled a scream. Apes on horseback broke through the trees and raced straight toward Luc. They were armored, like all ape soldiers, and they wore tall helmets on their heads. They hooted and roared as they saw the human standing in the middle of the clearing. In a rush of hooves, the riders thundered toward Luc. The human cried out in alarm and raised his arms to ward off their blows. Daena covered her eyes, not wanting to see the deathblow. A second later the rumble of hooves faded.

Daena looked up. The flying sticks had been trampled into the dust. Luc was gone.

"What the—!" Birn started to yell.

Pak dove at him, clamping a hand over the other boy's mouth. Pak held a finger up to his mouth and pointed out into the forest. The fear in his eyes told Daena everything. *They're still out there.*

She listened, and a moment later she heard a horse snort somewhere through the trees. She couldn't see them, but she could hear them, and that meant they could hear her if she made too much noise. Apes had sharp senses, and they were incredibly fast.

"We've got to get out of here," she whispered, so softly that she could barely hear herself.

Birn nodded. Pak took his hands away, and all three of them stood up. A dozen questions filled Daena's mind. What was an ape patrol doing so far from the city? Why

had they swooped down on Luc so quickly? Were they looking for more humans?

Daena's mother, Sarai, was the leader of the clan, and
she had chosen to make their camp close to Ape City. But
not too close. Humans very rarely saw apes unless they
ventured toward the walls, and when apes did come close
to the clan's camp, it was usually by accident—lost patrols,
or ape citizens out exploring, or caravans on their way to
other ape cities beyond the mountains. But this ape patrol
hadn't looked lost. They'd charged forward with a purpose
and nearly yanked Luc right out of his moccasins. If the
apes were expanding their patrols, the clan had to know
about it right away before any more humans were attacked.

"Let's go," she said.

Staying low, the three human children turned their
backs on the clearing and crept deeper into the woods.
They heard the sound of an ape voice barking a short command, and once the heavy thud of a horse hoof on damp
ground, but otherwise the forest was silent. They reached
the path, still hearing nothing. Even though there was no
noise, a sense of apprehension filled the air, and Pak
motioned for them to remain silent. Daena nodded and
pointed across the bare ground to the line of trees on the
far side. Pak went first, glancing left and right, then dash-
ing across the open space and slipping into the bushes as
smoothly as a snake. Even though she was only a few feet
from him, Daena barely heard him move.

Birn was next. He moved more like a bull than a snake,

but he made no noise, and a moment later he was gone. Daena stood up slowly and took a step out onto the path.

Snap.

Her foot landed on the twig. The sound of it breaking shot through the quiet forest like a scream. Daena froze. For a split second after her step there was no sound, and she thought she might get away with it. But as she took her second step she felt the ground tremble beneath her feet.

"Run!" Birn shouted from the woods.

Two apes came around a bend in the forest path, riding side by side. In a split second they were close enough that she could see their black, shining eyes and the wide, flaring nostrils on their flat noses. The riders roared, baring their fangs. One rider leaned to his left, the other to his right, arm outstretched. They were going to scoop her up, whichever way she went.

Daena didn't go sideways—she went forward. Diving straight ahead, the human girl slid right between the two horses, surprising the apes and landing on her hands and knees behind the horses before they could even slow down. Jumping to her feet, Daena scrambled into the woods, thrashing her way through a thick bush, then sprinted without slowing down. Birn and Pak fell in beside her, all hope of silence gone, all three of them running for their lives. Almost immediately they heard the sounds of pursuit. The apes had abandoned their horses and were sprinting after them through the trees. Apes moved fast, both on the ground and among the treetops.

Humans did not escape apes by running. Humans did not escape apes by fighting. Humans escaped apes by luck, and only luck.

Daena shook her head. That's what the clan said. It's not what her mother said, and her mother was the smartest person Daena knew. *You can outthink them.* That's what her mother said. Apes know a lot of things, but that didn't mean they were smarter. *Brains are measured by what you do with your circumstances.*

Daena heard leaves shake above her. When she looked up, there was nothing, but she knew that one of the apes had taken to the trees. It would come at them from above. Still at a dead run, she snatched at a low-hanging branch and snapped it off the trunk of a tree. The tree's leaves were thin and pointed like tiny needles. She shook it once to test its strength. The branch was supple, but strong.

"Not going to scare them with that," Birn panted beside her.

"Don't need to scare them," Daena replied.

They kept running. Behind them, the sounds of pursuit grew louder, and they came from the left. The three young humans veered right, trying to gain more distance. Herding us, Daena thought. She gripped her little club more tightly.

Suddenly, an ape dropped headfirst from the treetops, thick arms outstretched. Upside down, the armored gorilla grabbed Birn in its hands and started to haul him upward. Birn shouted and fought back, but his arms were pinned by a creature with three times his strength. Daena jabbed her tree branch forward, shoving the sharp nettles into the gorilla's face. The ape howled and dropped Birn, trying to push the branch off its face. But Daena shoved it harder, snapping the ape's head back. The soldier lost his balance, and his feet lost their grip on the branch overhead. The ape hit the ground hard and didn't move again.

The three humans kept running and didn't look back.

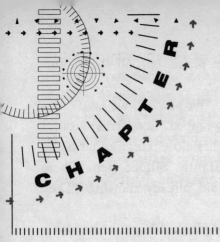

THREE

Exhausted and bruised, the three human teens crawled back into the clan's camp. It was only three miles from Luc's clearing to the little valley where the clan pitched its tents, but Daena and her friends had covered half the distance at a dead run and the other half at a slow, cautious pace that was even more tiring. Accidentally leading ape soldiers to the clan's camp was the worst mistake a human could make. The only reason the offense wasn't punished by death was that the error usually meant death for everyone at the camp.

Daena, Birn, and Pak staggered into the outer circle of animal skin tents and found a small group waiting for them. Daena saw her mother, Sarai, whose hair was as dark and straight as Daena's was blond. Her father, Karubi, was there, too. His coloring matched hers, and marked them both as people from the plains beyond the mountains.

"M-mother!" Daena gasped. "We saw . . . we saw."

"Apes," Sarai said. She wrapped her arms around Daena's shoulders and hugged her close. Her mother had a smooth, gentle voice that instantly calmed her. "There were apes in the forest," Sarai said, already knowing. "They captured someone."

"Luc," Birn spoke up. "They plucked him like he was a weed."

"I know," Daena's mother said. Daena didn't know how she knew, but Sarai had always seemed to know everything. "But I don't think they're following you. I had watchers in the forest, and they spotted you." She looked meaningfully at Daena. "Are you all right? Is anyone hurt?"

"No, we're fine."

"Good. Because if you were hurt, I'd have a harder time being so angry at you." Sarai's voice hardened into stone, and she pushed Daena away just far enough to look her in the eye. "I don't ever want to hear about your going off into the woods alone again. It's not safe."

"I know it's not safe!" Daena said. "But nowhere's safe around here. The apes are patrolling farther and farther from the city. We need to move."

Sarai hesitated. "We're not moving."

"Why not?" Daena asked. "We're too close to Ape City as it is. We don't need to be here. Why don't we just find a new place to live?"

"Because Sarai is stubborn."

The new voice that spoke came out of the brush, and as Daena turned she saw a man step out, half covered in leaves and twigs, his face coated with dust. He was short and thick, like the stump of a tree, and his face was half hidden by a thick beard. He looked very much like Pak would look when the boy was older—which made sense, because this was Pak's father, Vasich. Vasich was a squat, broad-shouldered man with hair even darker than Sarai's. He had been the leader of a clan of wildings who lived in the area. Most of them had joined Sarai's band as soon as she moved in. Vasich had gone along grudgingly.

Vasich brushed leaves from his body. They were from a tree the wildings called a "rain tree" because its leaves smelled strongly of damp bark after a long rain. The wildings used it to mask their scent when they were hiding from ape patrols. "Stupid to live here. Stupid not to find shelter in the rain, stupid not to go where apes are not."

Sarai had heard all this before. "You wildings didn't think so when we first came to this land. Your people were talking about fighting the apes back then."

"That was stupid, too," Vasich agreed. "But Vasich was not clan leader then."

"Vasich is not clan leader now," Sarai reminded him. "I am."

Vasich grunted but said nothing. A year ago, Sarai had led her people over the mountains and into this forest a few miles from Ape City. They had come looking for food, and they'd settled in land already belonging to a clan of wild-ings. Some of the wildings had foolishly tried to attack the apes and been killed. After having their own run-in with the apes, Sarai's people had established this camp and many of the wildings had joined them. Vasich had been one of these, but he'd never really accepted Sarai's rule as his law.

"Stupid rules," Vasich grumbled. "Stupid things to say, saying to live so close to the flat noses. And for what? Because you think it will make them like us! Bah!" The wilding spat. "They hunt us. They take us in nets. They drag us back to their city. That's what we get for living here."

"There is a way," Sarai said for the hundredth time. "There is a way for us to live with apes. We can't just fight them, and we can't just run away. We humans deserve a life that is better than this, but we'll only be able to find it when we live in peace with the—"

"Words!" Vasich snorted. "Always so many words. You have the dark hair of a wilding, but you use the big words of a tek. I think it spins your brain in your head. I'm tired of hearing all your words."

A few of the clansmen grumbled unhappily, and beside Sarai, Karubi shifted his grip on his thick walking stick. But he didn't move. This was Sarai's fight to accept or ignore.

"You will keep hearing them," Sarai said, not backing down from Vasich, "as long as you are part of this clan."

Vasich shook his head, his wild black hair shaking around his face. "Not the only choice. I stay. We have new leader." He looked around at the others. They were mostly teks, but there were a few wildings scattered among them. All of them sensed the direction he was going. None of their expressions looked encouraging. But Vasich didn't care. He turned his eyes back to Sarai. "I challenge the chief of the clan."

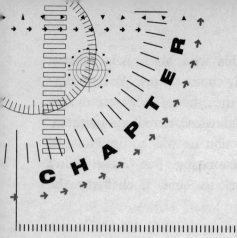

"Father, why don't you do something?" Daena whispered.

She and her father were watching as Vasich and Sarai stared at each other. Vasich had uttered his challenge and was waiting for Sarai to respond.

Karubi never took his eyes off Vasich, but he shook his head and said softly, "It's not the way this is done, Daena. Sarai is strong in her mind. She became clan chief through her wits. She has to use her wits to keep her place. That's how it works. It has to work that way."

"But what if he hurts her?"

Karubi said, "Then I'll kill him."

Sarai kept her eyes fixed on Vasich, studying him coldly as he waited for her response. Finally, she said, "I accept the challenge."

"I want the three tests," Vasich said quickly, his words coming right on top of hers. "I want them now."

Karubi motioned for Daena to stay put, and he moved toward Sarai. At the same time, Birn stepped closer to the girl. "Your mother has been clan chief for as long as I can remember. What are the three tests? Are they going to fight?"

"She told me once," Daena explained. "It's how someone challenges the chief. They have three tests. Each test has to be connected to the one before somehow. Like, the tests are done in the same place, or they use the same object in each test. Something like that."

"What are the tests?"

"The challenger gets to decide," Daena said. "But then for each test, the chief gets to add something to put the test in their favor. That's so things are fair."

"Test now!" Vasich demanded.

"You're the challenger," Sarai said. "Name your test."

Vasich looked around until he spotted a large stone half buried in the dirt. He grabbed it in both hands and rocked it back and forth until it broke loose from the dirt, then he lifted it. The stone was about the size of a melon, almost round, and gray. It looked heavy. The wilding searched the ground until he found another stone of equal size and dug that one up, too. Vasich grinned. "I chose a contest of strength."

"No kidding," Daena whispered.

"Whoever can hold these stones outstretched in his arms is the winner," he explained. And with that, he stretched out his hands, balancing the stones.

"Wait," Karubi grunted. "The chief has a say in the test."

The dark-haired wilding shrugged. "Say."

Sarai pursed her lips. She struggled to find some way to alter this contest. It was obvious that she couldn't beat Vasich in a contest of strength. He was as strong as a tree with arms as thick and hard as roots. But the wilding was clever enough to have chosen a simple test. She couldn't think of anything to do to change it.

"Enough time. I go," Vasich declared. He held the stones out away from his body. Then he locked his eyes on Sarai and grinned. Karubi began to tap his walking stick into the ground, counting out the time. The staff had punched a hole in the ground before Vasich's arm began to tremble, and Karubi had dug a small pit by the time the wilding grunted and let his arm lower. Then, as if to show Sarai just how strong he was, he handed her the stones by holding them out to her with arms extended, untrembling.

Sarai took the stones without comment. "Count," she said to her husband. She held out her arms.

She did not hold it out for long. Her arms collapsed almost immediately. The gathered clan murmured in disappointment. The first test had gone to Vasich.

"Hah!" the wilding gloated. "Second test. Who can carry the stones overhead while walking around the village more times." Daena felt her heart skip a beat. Vasich was going to keep picking contests of strength. Sarai would never beat him that way.

The wilding hefted the stones. "Wait," Sarai said. The eyes of the clan watched her hopefully. "The test will be what you say," she declared. "But I add this. We will see who can carry the stone overhead while walking around the village more times after the stone has sat in the fire for as long as you held it up."

The clan murmured admiringly. Daena, too, saw the cleverness in Sarai's idea. With the time, she had connected the second test more closely with the first, which meant Vasich couldn't complain. Putting the stone in the fire would give her a chance to rest her arm. But this test was no longer a contest of strength. It was a test of willpower.

The clan always kept at least one fire burning in camp. Karubi took the stones and carried them to the flame. He dropped them in and then began to count out the passage of time. When he had reached the same number he'd reached earlier, he motioned to Vasich. The wilding gritted his teeth and approached the fire reluctantly. With a growl, he reached in and snatched the rocks up in his hands. The stones glowed a dull red and smoked. Moving at nearly a sprint, the wilding hurried to the edge of the camp and started walking. But he'd hardly gone a dozen steps before he howled and dropped the stones, waving his hands as though to shake the pain out of them.

"Agh," he growled, blowing on his hands. "You cannot do this."

Sarai said nothing. She walked over to him and slowly picked up the stones. They had cooled off somewhat, but they were still warm. Sarai kept her expression steady as she dropped the stones back into the fire. "Count," she said.

Karubi tapped his walking stick again, its pace slow as a steady heartbeat. Sarai never looked at the stones. She kept as cool as the rocks were hot, sometimes studying Vasich coldly, sometimes glancing at the members of her clan, totally unconcerned about the test. When her husband stopped his counting, Sarai reached into the fire and grabbed both stones and lifted them over her head. Smoke rose up from her clenched fists. Her arms trembled more than Vasich's had, but it was the weight of the stones that made her shake, not their heat. Sarai set her jaw and walked—she did not run, she walked—to the edge of the camp. Then with slow, deliberate steps, she traced a circle around the gathering of tents. By the rules, she had won the contest after only a few steps, because Vasich had not made it that far. But she completed her circle anyway, to the cheers of her clan.

Sarai dropped the stones at Vasich's feet and said simply, "I win that one." Daena looked at her mother's hands and saw blisters there. Sarai herself ignored them.

Vasich snorted. "Third test!" He reached down to grab the stones. The crowd laughed when he stopped short, touching them first to make sure they were cool. Then he lifted them. "Who can throw the stones highest and keep them in the air longest."

Sarai hesitated. Then she grinned. "Agreed. Here is my

change. Who can keep throw the stones high enough to count all the members of the clan."

The wilding chewed his lower lip as his mind worked over her challenge. "You say the most members of the clan, or all members."

"All members."

Daena glanced around. They were a large clan, with at least forty people. Who could throw two stones high enough to count to forty? What was her mother trying to do?

"We will both fail that one," Vasich said. The clan murmured their agreement. They were as confused as Daena was.

"If we both fail," Sarai said, "then you can choose another test, and I will give up my right to change it."

The murmuring grew louder and more concerned. Without Sarai's right to change, Vasich would simply choose another contest of strength and win the leadership of the clan. Sarai was risking everything on a test that neither of them could win.

The wilding shrugged. He picked up both stones and weighed them in his hands. Then he took a deep breath, crouched low, and hurled the two rocks underhanded into the air. As they sailed up, Vasich immediately began pointing at clan members, counting as fast as he could. "One-twothreefourfivesix . . . " Numbers spilled out of his mouth. He had thrown the rocks high, and he counted fast, but he had reached only up to twenty when the two stones thudded back to the ground.

Vasich looked unconcerned. "Maybe you can count faster, but you cannot throw higher. You will fail, too, and then I will be chief."

"Will you?" Sarai said.

She walked over and picked up the stones. Like Vasich, she balanced them in her hands, feeling their weight. Then, with a windup, she launched them into the air. Everyone could see they would not go as high as Vasich's toss had taken them. Everyone heard Sarai begin to count.

By fives.

"Five, ten, fifteen, twenty, twenty-five, thirty, thirty-five, forty."

She was done. The stones hit the ground.

"No!" Vasich roared. "Unfair! That was not the whole clan!"

Sarai shrugged. "It was the whole clan. There are forty in our clan. I counted to forty."

"But not each one!"

"I did not say to count each one. I said to count them all. I did that. I win."

Vasich opened his mouth to protest, but he choked on his own words. The clan, silent for a moment, erupted in cheers. None of them had guessed at the cleverness of Sarai's ruse.

"No, no, no!" the wilding complained, his voice rising above the praise of the others. "I challenge again!"

Before Sarai could reply, Karubi stepped forward. Although slimmer than Vasich, he was taller and still very muscular. He glared at the wilding with violence in his eyes. "The challenge is done. You cannot challenge again. That is the rule." Karubi wore an eager look, as though he hoped that Vasich would argue. But Vasich glanced from the taller man to the faces of the clan, and he saw how much they were against him. He lowered his shoulders and backed away. "You are following a fool," he said to them. "Follow her and you will all end up stuck to the ends of ape spears."

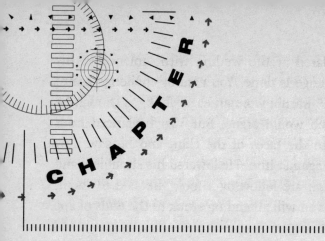
"It's been two weeks since anyone saw an ape."

"But two people vanished before that. Remember Tarik, Suni's boy? Gone."

"And some of the wildings from the clan beyond the low hills. They say they've lost people, too."

"We have to live somewhere."

"But not here. There are other places with food, but no apes."

That was the talk around the council fire two weeks after Sarai survived as chief. She sat cross-legged before the fire, with Karubi and six other teks all helping to form a circle. They talked over the fire, their words passing through licks of flame and plumes of sparks. Sarai encouraged these meetings. She encouraged her people to voice their opinions. She had learned to be a leader from her father, who had been chief of this tek tribe long before her. He had taught her that a true leader acted as first among equals—confident in guiding others but never talking down to them. The meetings around the fire gave her a chance to listen to their concerns and to explain her decisions.

The others had been talking as the moon sailed from one end of the sky to the other. Their talk was mostly of the apes and of the humans who had disappeared. There was no denying that ape patrols were out there hunting humans. Every human in the clan knew how cruelly apes could treat the species they despised. But there was something different about the patrols lately—they weren't just trying to drive humans out of ape territory. They were laying traps. Catching humans.

The other council members finally stopped talking and turned to Sarai. She looked each of them in the eye, one by one, until finally her gaze rested on Karubi. His eyes smiled at her. She always found comfort in her husband. Strong and smart, he could have been chief himself, but he deferred to her and her vision of a future for the human race.

"A time will come," she said simply, "when apes will not send patrols against us. They will send armies. Most apes just think of us as pests, but some want us destroyed."

The elders around her could only nod in agreement. A season ago, the apes had visited some ancient ruins and uncovered a terrible plague. They had tried to spread the plague among the humans to wipe them out, but the plan backfired. The sickness affected only apes, and Ape City itself was saved only because Sarai and a young female chimp had worked together.

Sarai continued. "The clans will have only two choices. Either we can learn to fight them, or learn to live with them so that day never comes. I do not believe we can ever fight the apes. They are stronger, faster—"

"—and smarter," said Mellie. Many years and many sorrows were woven together on her face.

"Not smarter," Sarai insisted. "They know more than we do, but they are not smarter. We can be smart, but not as long as we spend our days in fear of the apes. We must live in safety, and to do that we must make peace with them."

"I agree," said another elder. This was Ark, a man with a wise brain and a sharp tongue. "I definitely agree. So let's march down to Ape City and declare peace. See what happens then." He snorted at his own joke and folded his arms across his chest.

Sarai sighed. "I don't say I have all the answers. But I do know that the farther we stay from apes, the more they will hate us. Unless they can see that we can make things, that we raise families, that we care for one another, they'll see us only as animals. They'll hunt us."

"They're hunting us now!" Mellie insisted. "We could move back into the mountains; we could go back to the plains where there are no apes—"

"And no food," Karubi pointed out.

"And no food," Sarai agreed. "But what would we do then? Live for a time until the apes build a city there, and then be driven out again to go somewhere else. And then move again and again as the apes grow stronger. Someday we'll have to face them in some corner of the world. It might as well be here."

Outside Sarai's tent, three figures huddled among the shadows, listening. As the council meeting broke up, they slipped away from the tent to their own quiet, watchful spot.

"I'm sorry, Daena, but your mother is wrong," Birn said.

"Wrong to death, maybe," Pak agreed.

"That's your father talking," Daena snapped at the wilding. "I can't believe he tried to take the clan from my mother."

Pak looked sheepish. He had been embarrassed by his father's challenge and humiliated when he lost. "He . . . he was only trying to do what he thought was best."

"She's not wrong. My mother is never wrong," Daena declared.

Birn shook his head. "Apes and humans will never live in peace because humans will always fear apes."

"And apes are smarter," Pak added. "Even smarter than teks."

"You're the ones who are wrong," Daena said defensively. "You see a flat-nosed hairy face, and you're scared right out of your skins."

"And you're not?" Birn replied. "I saw your face when the apes nearly caught us the other day."

"And I saved your hide, too. Apes aren't so dangerous. I bet I could walk up and touch the walls of Ape City itself." She snapped a finger to show how easy it would be.

"Yeah?" Birn said. "Then do it."

"Huh?"

"To show how easy it is. How smart humans can be. If you're right—"

"—if your mother's right," Pak added.

"—then it shouldn't be any problem for you."

"Um, Daena, you know we were kidding."

Night had nearly passed into morning. It had taken the three youths two hours to hike to the plain that surrounded Ape City. Pak and Birn had gone only reluctantly, helplessly following Daena's stubborn lead.

The minute Birn had dared her, Daena knew what she must do. She would meet this challenge just as Sarai had met her challenge. Daena was her mother's daughter, and she would not back down from anyone. So she had leaped to her feet and started off. Fortunately, like most humans she knew the woods by night and day, and with the moon nearly full it was easy enough to walk through the woods at night. There were fewer ape patrols at night, which made it even easier to creep down to the flat lands.

Before them lay the great open space that the apes had cleared between their city and the forest. Anyone who wanted to approach Ape City had to cross that barren, coverless stretch of land, naked and exposed to the skies above. If an ape patrol spotted her, there would be nowhere to run, nowhere to hide.

Daena felt her knees quiver, but she kept her voice steady. "Were you?" she said casually. "I wasn't. I'm going to go up and touch the walls of the city. You want to come?"

Pak shook his head. "No. Why would I—"

Birn elbowed him in the ribs. "If you go, we'll go. Just lead the way, little chief."

Daena grinned. She could see why her mother liked being chief. It was exciting to get people to follow her. "We'll be fine if we go slow and low. And when we get back, we can tell everyone."

She hesitated a moment longer. Out on the plain there was no movement. Under the last of the moonlight they could see a few buildings—farms or lonely homesteads—but very little else. Apes were group creatures, Daena knew. Even more than humans, they liked to live together. This late at night it was unlikely that they would meet any stray apes on the plains. But if they met a patrol, they were in trouble.

Encouraged by the silence, Daena moved slowly out of the tree line and into the open, staying low and hurrying forward. Almost immediately she had a sense of helplessness, like a turtle suddenly turned on its back. But she kept going. She would prove to her friends, and to her mother's rivals, that humans did not need to fear apes.

As she moved across the flats, Daena felt a sense not of fear but of wonder. Before her stood Ape City, a walled collection of houses and towers, twinkling with tiny lights like a chunk of heaven that had fallen to Earth. Even in the distance and darkness, she could see bridges that hung between the towers, and lights beaming from the tops of the spires, as clear and as bright as stars. She had grown up knowing nothing but dust and tents. To her, this city appeared almost magical.

As she approached, Daena instinctively moved toward whatever cover she could find. In places, fields of tall grass swept across large patches of land, and she and her friends moved through those slowly. In another area, they found a ditch like a dry riverbed, and crept along it for nearly two hundred yards. At the end of the ditch, Daena was about to climb out onto open ground when she heard a horse snort. She dropped low, nearly landing on top of Pak, and pressed a finger to her mouth.

Horse hooves clomped slowly toward them through the darkness, and they heard the faint clang of metal bumping gently against metal. Soldiers on horseback. They were moving slowly, lazily, like watchmen who worked a regular beat.

"You still up for that promotion?" one ape said.

Another ape drawled, "I think I got passed over. It isn't fair. Fall asleep on duty one time, and it's on your record for—hey, you smell something?"

The horse hooves stopped. Daena pressed herself into the dirt. The apes were close enough that she could hear them sniffing the air.

"I smell human stink," one of the apes said.

"Me, too," said the second. "But it's everywhere these days. They're bringing in slaves by the cartload now. Half the city stinks of 'em. Come on. Once more around the city, and we're done with our duty."

The other ape grunted, and the horse hooves clomped again. Daena waited until they were long gone before she sat up. "Close," she said under her breath.

Birn and Pak nodded. "Too close," Birn said. "Forget it. I'm not going any farther. This was a dumb idea."

"You're not up to it?" Daena teased.

"Neither are you. Come on, Daena, I'm sorry I said anything. It was just to poke fun at you. Let's go back."

"Not when I'm this close. Look, the walls are right there. Ten more minutes and we could touch it and go. Do you know anyone who's ever done that before? Come on, it'll take some of the mystery out of the apes. Make them seem less unbeatable."

"They are unbeatable," Pak said. "Go now."

"Then wait here," Daena insisted stubbornly. "I'll be back in a minute."

Before they could respond, she was rolling up and out of the ditch, on her feet, and moving forward. The walls of the city loomed overhead, taller than any hand-built thing she had ever seen in her life. Watch fires burned here and there along the length of the wall, but Daena couldn't see any soldiers walking between them. They probably were not guarded unless the apes were at war with each other. Even a hundred clans fighting together would not be able to break through that wall.

Even though she could see no guards, Daena covered the last few yards as quietly as a fish gliding through deep water. She reached the wall and pressed herself against it. She'd done it. She was touching the wall of Ape City itself—the home of the race that hated and hunted hers. She flushed, and the stones felt cool against her suddenly warm skin. It was hard to believe that any creature could make a wall so enormous. Compared to this, the tents of the clans were pathetic and primitive, the work of smaller brains and weaker hands. Daena thought of her mother's saying, that apes were not really smarter, and for the first time she doubted it.

Daena stood there a moment longer, savoring her secret victory. Just as she was about to peel herself off the wall and start back, a small horn blared, and nearby a gate swung open. The girl choked back a cry and crouched down, wishing she could pull shadows around her like a blanket. Torches appeared, bobbing up and down. In their light she could see a short column of apes, twenty in all, stomping out of the small gate and heading out onto the plains.

They've seen us! was Daena's panicked thought. But the apes were advancing with no real hurry and no particular purpose. They moved with the same businesslike boredom that the two riders had, and she guessed that they were yet another patrol. If she lay quietly for a moment, and stuck to the darkest shadows at the foot of the wall, she would be safe.

She felt an even greater sense of relief wash over her when the small column of soldiers moved farther away from the wall, not even glancing in her direction. The bright torchlight quickly shrank into small points of light as the apes marched forward. As soon as they were gone, she would be able to leave the wall and—

Daena's heart sank. She had wanted to sprint back to the ditch when it was safe. But the apes were headed right for the ditch. They were headed right for Birn and Pak.

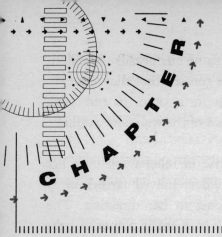

CHAPTER SIX

The two boys watched from the ditch as the apes approached.

"No, no, no, no," Pak whispered, his voice becoming more panicked with each repetition of the word. Birn felt the other boy trembling violently. Wildings, he knew, always reacted violently to apes. They seemed to hate apes even more than teks, and they were also far more terrified of them. Pak, accustomed to the forest, probably felt especially vulnerable being out in the open.

"We've got to run," Birn said.

"No, they'll see us," Pak hissed. "Movement is easy to see."

"*We're* easy to see if we just stay here. They're coming this way! Come on!"

Pak shook his head, sheer terror in his eyes.

Birn looked up. It was too late. The apes were nearly at the ditch. The minute Birn raised himself up from the ground he'd be spotted.

"Hey!" A voice called out from the wall. A girl's voice. "Hey, you fat, hairy, flat-faced fools! Over here!"

The apes stopped. As one they turned away, suddenly alert. Their routine early morning march had just turned into anything but routine.

Birn sat up, now looking at the backs of the apes. Far beyond them, he could hear Daena's voice. "Come and get me, you thick-skulled bristle-backed bullies!"

Birn couldn't believe his ears. Daena was distracting the apes, trying to give her friends time to escape back into the forest. The apes murmured, and one of them barked an order. The whole squad started to double-time back toward the wall, fanning out into a search formation. They moved with practiced speed. There was no way Daena would escape them. Birn felt the urge to run—but he couldn't just abandon Daena like that.

"No, over here!" he shouted. His voice cracked with fear, but he shouted even louder, "You slack-jawed knuckle-draggers!"

Pak looked at him as though he was insane.

The apes turned back, shocked by the sound of the second voice. They looked confused. The last thing in the world they had expected was to hear two human voices taunting them only a few feet from the walls of their own city.

"Come on!" Birn said, feeling triumphant. "Let's go!"

He dragged Pak to his feet, and the two boys started to run.

But this wasn't a forest game. For all the names the humans had thrown, these were not slack-jawed, thick-skulled fools. They were professional soldiers, and most of them were gorillas—the best fighters in apedom. A few quickly shouted orders turned their confusion into action. Instantly the apes split into two columns, one advancing toward the wall and the other turning back to charge toward the ditch.

Pak let out a wordless shriek and ran. Birn followed him, running the length of the ditch and then scrambling up onto level ground. A roar from the apes told him they'd been spotted. He didn't look back. The human boy kept his eyes on the darkness in front of him. Somewhere ahead lay the tree line, and safety. He forced his feet to move faster. Pak ran ahead of him, smaller, lighter, and faster. His little legs churned faster than bird wings, and he quickly gained ground.

Pak's going to make it, Birn thought. Pak will make it to the trees and I'll get caught.

He didn't hear the horses until too late. At the last minute Birn had a sense of them—thundering hooves charging toward him. Two ape riders exploded out of the darkness, scooping up Pak, then disappearing into the darkness once again. Birn heard the wilding boy shriek. Then the cry was cut short, and he was gone. Birn stumbled but didn't fall. He kept running, hearing the apes closing in behind him. He ran blindly, terrified. Then something slapped him in the face, soft but sharp, and then again, and he realized he was running among the low-hanging branches of trees. Somewhere behind him, apes howled their frustration.

He ran hard and noisily for another few hundred feet, then, instinctively, he stopped. His heart pounded like a drum. His lungs screamed for air, but he held his breath and listened. He could hear apes thrashing through the trees, roaring and howling, trying to scare him into bolting. But he knew there weren't enough of them. Apes moved quickly through the forest, but even they couldn't see through bushes and leaves, and the darkness gave him even more cover. If he could keep his head, he just might survive.

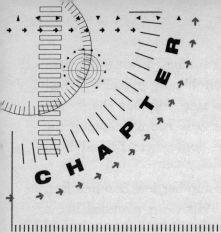

SEVEN

Hot, stinking breath. Thick, hairy arms as hard as rocks. Sharp claws. That was all Daena felt. An explosion of angry sounds and violent gestures as apes swarmed around her, fast and cruel, shoving her to the ground. A big gorilla snarled in her face, warning her not to make any trouble, and she felt all strength leave her limbs.

The speed with which they'd attacked her was frightening. She had known the risk when she called out, but she thought at least she'd be able to run, or find someplace to hide. But she'd hardly taken four steps before they were on her, a dozen of them, five times as strong as Vasich. Her hands were tied, and a moment later she was thrown over one ape's shoulder like a sack of wheat. Her head swam, and it hurt. She might have hit it on the ground—she didn't know. In a daze, she felt herself being carried for only a few minutes, but it must have been longer, because when she opened her eyes again she was inside the city, and the darkness had turned to light gray as the sun began to rise somewhere far away. Every time she tried to lift her head she felt dizzy, so she saw nothing of the Ape City except for paths that were made of stone rather than dirt and buildings made of wood and stone, with many stories and many windows. Apes were all around her, most of them laughing, some of them curious, as the ape soldiers told the story of their curious patrol.

Then, before she knew it, Daena felt the bonds on her wrists suddenly cut. She was set on her feet and then shoved backward. She stumbled over something and fell to the ground.

"Hey!"

"Watch it!"

"Get off me!"

Daena found herself sitting among humans, all of whom had been lying on a straw-covered floor, sleeping. She blinked and looked around. In the growing light she could see that she was in a large cage, like a holding pen, with metal bars from floor to ceiling.

"Get off me!"

Daena shifted away from the nearest human, who propped himself up on his arms and blinked at her. Tears welled up in her eyes, and Daena stifled a sob. The human rubbed his face and then said gruffly, "You just get caught?"

Daena nodded.

"Aw, you're just a kid. I'm sorry. Hey, Mai, they just brought in a little girl."

A female human sat up. Like the man she looked exhausted, but she also appeared instantly sympathetic. She touched a hand to Daena's shoulder. "Did they hurt you?"

Daena shook her head. "I . . . I don't think so. I hit my head, but I'm okay."

"I don't know you, little one. What is your clan?"

"Our chief is Sarai. We came from over the mountains last year."

The woman nodded. "I know your people. We traded animal pelts with your clan just before the cold season." She frowned and brushed a hair from Daena's face. "There are many from your clan here. Your chief stays too close to the ape places."

Daena bristled. "You're here, too."

The man said, "You speak true. But apes came from far away to raid our camp, and most of our clan escaped. Half your people are here. They brought another one in just before you."

The man pointed at a small figure curled up on the floor. It was Pak. "Did they . . . did they bring in any more? Another boy?"

"No," the woman said.

Daena felt a glimmer of hope warm her. At least Birn had escaped. "What . . . will they do with me? Will we . . . are they going to kill us?"

The woman shook her head. "No. Not right away."

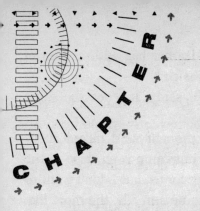

CHAPTER

EIGHT

The sun had risen over the mountains, warming the tents of Sarai's clan and rousing her people. Sarai herself was already awake, gathering food and tools and stuffing them into a leather sack. Karubi was helping her, but he worked with a distinctly unhappy look on his face.

Finally, he said, "I don't think you should go."

Sarai nodded. "I know."

"But you're going to the mountains anyway."

She nodded. "I don't trust any of the wildings to do it, and I'm the only one in the clan who knows the mountains. It makes sense."

Her husband shrugged. "Maybe. But it doesn't make sense for you to leave with Vasich and the other wildings making so much trouble. You are the chief of the clan. You should be here."

Sarai closed the top of her leather bag with a strip of animal hide. "You can handle Vasich."

"I could kill Vasich," Karubi said. "It's not the same thing."

Sarai stopped her work. "I thought we'd talked about this. The clan is unhappy that our camp is so close to the apes. I want to find a better place for us, but I don't want to keep moving. The more we become nomads, the more like wildings we will be. Civilization means finding a permanent place to live. I'm going up into the mountains to find one."

Karubi sighed. "Maybe it's just because I'm going to miss you. Last time you were away, you were nearly killed by apes. You need me around to keep you out of trouble."

She kissed him on the cheek. "That's for sure. But at least I know that as long as you're here, everything will be fine."

"Help!"

Husband and wife nearly jumped off their feet as the cry ripped through the still morning air. They saw the young boy Birn running exhausted through the camp, hurrying toward them. His face, arms, and legs were streaked with sweat and grime.

"Help," he said again, his breath ragged and short. "He—"

"What's wrong?" Sarai said. Karubi was already scanning the trees where Birn had appeared, looking for signs of trouble.

"D-D-Daena . . . Pak . . . they . . . caught."

Sarai's heart froze in her chest. "Caught? The apes?"

Other clan members stumbled out of their tents, alarmed by the cries.

Birn nodded. "We went to the city—"

"You what!"

"It-it was a dare. . . . "

"You never go near that place. Never!" Karubi snapped.

Vasich had come out of his tent, bleary-eyed and irritable. "Someone went to the ape city?"

"Daena and . . . and Pak," Birn admitted.

"My son!" The blood drained from Vasich's face. "They killed my son?"

Birn swallowed hard. "I . . . I don't know if they're dead. I think they were captured."

Vasich howled . . . a long, anguished sound like the cry of a wolf. He tore hair from his head and beard and dropped to his knees. "My son!" he shouted. Then, as abruptly as his wailing had begun, it stopped. The wilding leaped to his feet, fire in his eyes. "I must get him."

"No." Sarai held up her hand to stop him.

"What? This is your fault. You bring us too close to their places! Because of you he is in there!"

"I won't let you go," she warned.

"You have me stay here? Forget my own son?"

"No," Sarai said firmly. "I want you to stay here while I go to the city."

"Sarai!" her husband said in shock. But Sarai held

firm. "You say it is my fault. Maybe, maybe not. You say that I'm a fool for trying to make peace with apes. That may be true, or not. But I can tell you this. There is an ape in the city who might help us. I will go and find her."

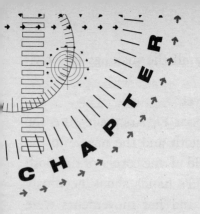

CHAPTER NINE

Ari smoothed the carefully brushed fur on her face and sighed. "Don't worry. You're learning rather quickly . . . for a human."

Behind her, a young human named El put her head down, embarrassed. She held a brush in her hand, clenched in her fist as if it were a meat cleaver. "I'm sorry, miss. I'm trying . . . "

"I know, I know," Ari said gently. "Brushing my fur is something new for you. I don't think any ape has ever let a human do it before. Let's try something else. Ah, the needle and thread."

The young chimpanzee stood up from her seat and walked over to a small end table. On it lay a needle, some thread, and cloth. As she picked up these items, Ari took a deep breath and reminded herself to be patient. Somewhere inside these humans lay all the makings of a civilized society.

She just hadn't found them yet.

When she turned back to poor El, Ari made sure she was smiling. She handed the cloth and the needle to the human confidently, but kept hold of one corner of the cloth to make sure it wouldn't fall. El's hands shook nervously when she was trying to sew, and her movements were always so clumsy that she often dropped the material. "Now, remember where we left off yesterday. Go gently with the design. Push the needle through slowly, make sure it follows the pattern . . . Ow!"

El had jabbed the needle hard through the cloth, slipping and piercing Ari's thumb. The chimp squealed and jammed her thumb into her mouth, jumping up and down in pain.

"I'm sorry, miss, I'm sorry!" the human squeaked, dropping the needle and thread. "Please don't punish me!"

Ari forced herself to calm down. El's frightened reaction made the chimp burn with shame—not for herself, but for all of apekind. She raised a hand, and El flinched, but Ari put the hand gently on the human girl's shoulder. "El, this is not the barn. I am not the stable master. I've told you, I hate how the overseers treat humans."

El was nearly sobbing, but she said, "Yes . . . yes, miss."

"I know it's hard for you to come into the house to work. I know the work is different. But you can learn, El. I know it. Humans can learn."

"It's not . . . miss, it's not what we're told in the stables." The girl sobbed between every word. Ari could see the frustration and fear in her. She would get no more out of this girl today.

"I think that's enough for now, El," Ari said softly. "Return to the kitchen, please. I think the cook has some cleaning for you after breakfast."

El turned away gratefully. As she hurried from the room, a small group of apes led by Ari's father, Sandar, entered. The human stepped out of the way, putting her head down instantly, as the newcomers passed by. Ari knew them all. Aside from her father, there came a massive gorilla with a broad silver back. This was General Krull, commander of the armies of the apes. Behind him walked a smaller figure, a chimp with fierce, keen eyes— Colonel Thade. Thade was walking beside an ape wearing the crimson robes of a priest of Semos. The priest was also wearing a red veil, but Ari guessed that it was Timon, the high priest himself. Timon and Thade were political allies and often combined their political muscle to get what they wanted. Behind them followed another big gorilla, but this one was younger, without even a speck of silver on his shoulders. His name was Attar, and he had been one of Ari's closest friends for as long as she could remember.

The other apes walked by the human without noticing, but Thade stopped and scowled at the human female who trembled in the corner. Then he looked at Ari.

"Still trying to work your magic, Ari?" said Colonel Thade. "If you succeed, let me know. I have a dog I would like to teach to polish my shoes."

Ari bristled. Colonel Thade was a frequent guest in her father's house, and she was forced to tolerate it. But it was difficult. "Humans are not dogs, Colonel."

"No," the military ape smirked. "Dogs can actually be taught."

Timon laughed, and even Attar and her father chuckled. But Ari did not back down. "Colonel, these humans are capable of a culture. They have intelligence. I know that— and so do you."

Thade stopped laughing. He glared at Ari with a fierceness that had terrified the toughest, most seasoned gorillas in the service. It was a look that promised violence. The colonel took a step forward, his upper lip curling. A chimp, he was not much taller than she, but the intensity of his personality made him seem twice his own size. He kept his eyes locked on Ari, but his words were addressed to her father. "Senator Sandar, you have my utmost respect, and I would not think of insulting your house with bad manners. But please remind your daughter that no one speaks to me that way."

Sandar gently inserted himself between them. "Ari, my dear, the colonel is a guest in our house. It's unseemly to act so rude."

Ari bowed her head to her father. She did not always agree with his politics, but she loved him dearly. And she knew that he indulged her. He was as gentle with her at home as he was fierce in the debate hall of the Senate. "I'm sorry, Father, but the colonel knows—"

Thade interrupted. "The colonel knows his own mind. No child should presume to tell me my business."

Ari fumed. She and Thade had had a run in last year when the plague had nearly entered their city. It was Ari who had gone to the humans to find a cure, and it was Ari who had brought back evidence of real human culture. But no one had listened to her, and what little evidence she discovered had disappeared. She knew Thade was involved—Thade and Timon. But she could prove nothing. Most apes considered humans little more than animals, and no one would listen to a young female.

"I'll prove that I'm right, Colonel," she said at last. "You know as well as I do that it was a human who showed us the plant medicine that cured the plague."

Thade nodded. "True. But even animals can sense a poisonous plant, or a good one. And many beasts can be taught tricks."

Timon pulled back his crimson veil and sniffed. "Indeed. There's no reason not to think a human could be taught a trick or two. But real knowledge? Ridiculous."

Thade moved past Ari dismissively. She looked from the colonel to General Krull to her father, but found no sympathy. Then she glanced at Attar, the young officer she had known since childhood. She caught a glimpse of something in his face. It wasn't sympathy, but it was a reaction.

"Attar?" she said softly, questioningly.

The young gorilla frowned and growled low. "Nothing, Ari. For once, leave it alone."

Then he turned and hurried after the others.

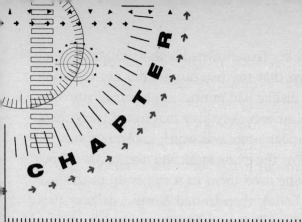

Sandar and the military apes were meeting on the porch, an elegant patio with walls and on either side two massive bayobab trees. Though it was daytime small lanterns hung from the branches; the candles they burned were not meant to light up the walkway, they burned a thick spice that drove away bugs.

Ari watched them move out onto the patio and frowned. Her father hadn't chosen the patio for the view. He had chosen it because it was the most private place in his house. For years, Sandar had held all his private meetings in a parlor on the other side of the house . . . until the day Ari, along with Attar, eavesdropped on them from the attic space above, and accidentally crashed down on the council.

Her father had moved his meetings to the patio, but Ari was nosy and stubborn, and the combination would not let her rest. Why had her father invited both Krull and Thade? It was well known that the two officers did not like each other—and their dislike had grown into a sort of smoldering disgust since last year. Anything that would bring them together under Sandar's roof was worth knowing about.

Ari walked across the living room and over to a wall covered with vines. She used them to scamper up to the second floor of the house, then trotted down a hallway to a small round window. The window did not give much of a view—it was built mainly to allow light into the hallway—so it was very small. But it was large enough for a female chimp to squeeze through. Ari popped the window open and wiggled herself out onto the roof of the house. The roof sloped, and there was no handrail, but Ari did not need one. No ape did. She hurried along the roof nimbly until she came over the top of the steepled house and then moved down the other side where the patio lay . . .

. . . only to find Attar standing there, waiting for her.

Ari looked at the big gorilla wearing his armored breastplate, his sword hanging at his hip. She had not spoken with him much in the last year, a year that had left its mark on the young soldier. Attar looked no bigger—if he got any bigger, he wouldn't fit through a door—but he did look older and more mature. Ari would have said "harder" or "meaner," if she still didn't think of him as a friend.

Before she could speak, Attar held up one hand. "Sorry, Ari, I have orders to stop you from eavesdropping this time."

Ari laughed. "That's funny. Last time you helped me listen in."

Attar didn't smile. "Last time I was a cadet in the academy. I was green. Now I'm a lieutenant with service under my belt. Things are different."

The female chimp sighed. "Things aren't different, Attar. You are. We hardly talk anymore, and you never visit."

Attar's professional soldier look cracked a little. "It wouldn't be right," he explained. "A junior officer visiting a senator. It goes against the chain of command."

"You're a family friend. Father sponsored you for the academy, for Semos's sake."

"Do not use that name in vain!" Attar said with sudden passion.

Ari took a step back, but immediately closed the distance again. She had known Attar too long to be afraid of his size. She studied his face. "You've become awfully religious lately—"

"There is nothing wrong with religion. A soldier knows his duty. It is the duty of every ape to worship Semos, the First Ape—"

"Yes, yes," Ari said, not wanting to be lectured to. "But not when it gets in the way of your friendships. You're becoming as obsessed with your religion as Timon the high priest."

"Timon," Attar snorted. "I can worship Semos without chasing after the skirts of that monkey in an ape suit."

Ari pointed toward the patio below them. "You wouldn't know that from the entrance you all made together. You look pretty friendly with all of them."

Attar growled. "I follow orders, Ari, not Timon. You know that. He was the meanest priest at the orphanage where I grew up, and I'll never forgive him for that. But General Krull is my commander, and I have great respect for Colonel Thade. And Thade, by the way, is very religious and a good soldier."

"Can you worship Semos and still think kindly about humans?" she asked, thinking of the smirk on his face earlier.

Attar frowned. "Humans are humans. They are beneath apes."

Ari sighed. "A human saved your life last year when you had the plague," she reminded him. "And in the middle of a fever dream, Semos visited you in a vision and told you that humans and apes should live in peace."

The young soldier shuffled from foot to foot nervously. He did not like to be reminded of those events last year. He had been infected with the deadly plague by Colonel Thade—an accident, the colonel had assured him—and only the combined efforts of Ari herself and a human named Sarai had saved him from certain death. "It was not Semos who visited me," Attar insisted. "It was the human. I was sick. She whispered poisons in my ear."

"That's Timon talking. Or Thade. You know the truth."

"Semos would never put humans on the same level as apes."

Ari shook her head. "When you say that, you sound like you're trying to convince yourself, not me."

Attar shuffled his feet again. Ari noticed how uncomfortable he looked. "That's it, isn't it?" she guessed. "You're trying to make yourself believe something you don't really believe. Something about humans. What is it?" When he did not reply, Ari pressed on. "A few minutes ago I said that humans were capable of learning, and I could tell you didn't like Thade's answer. What's going on, Attar? Why are they meeting?"

The young soldier growled low in his throat. "I'm an officer now, Ari. I won't tell you anything I've been ordered to keep secret."

"Attar," Ari chided.

Her old friend sighed. "Ari, it's nothing you'd be interested in. It's just something involving the building of the new Temple of Semos. That's all."

"A meeting that involves General Krull and Colonel Thade?" The female chimp shook her head. "I saw your face, Attar. This involves humans somehow."

Attar frowned. "I will tell you this." The gorilla leaned close, bowing his head to whisper close to her ear. "More and more humans are being carted into the city every day. Wild humans, controlled by slavers. And they are being taught things."

• • • • •

There was only one ape in the whole city who would take up the job of slave trader. And Ari knew just who it was.

A few hours later she had left her house and walked through the upscale neighborhoods of fashionable apes. Ape City was built on a hill, like most ape places, and the higher up one went, the better the neighborhoods became. The lower the altitude, the lower the living conditions of the apes. After twenty minutes of walking she left the trimmed yards and blossoming trees of her own district for the working-class neighborhoods down the hill. Here the houses were much smaller, with only one or two trees for climbing. The big, fan-leafed plants that were the main part of any well-tended garden on her block were thinner and smaller here, and some of them were turning brown. The worker apes didn't have much idle time to garden.

A few streets farther down the slope the houses gave way to shops and markets, and then the shops and markets disappeared, replaced by warehouses and piers. The streets, which were lined with cobblestones and flowered pots in her neighborhood, had narrowed to nothing more than muddy lanes. Higher up the hill, apes moved in and out of doors at a busy pace, paying social calls or buying goods from the markets. Down here life was a little slower paced. Artists and underemployed apes mingled. Apes sat on street corners and on the steps of empty, dark-windowed warehouses.

Ari walked past an ape dressed in little more than rags, huddled half beneath some tattered papers. It was a female. A tiny animal mewed on her lap.

"Spare a little something for a lass down on her luck?" the chimp said.

Ari felt a twinge of empathy. "A little . . . something?" Ari asked.

"You know, a bit of change, a small donation. Maybe the odd jewel or two."

"Yes, um, yes," she fumbled in her pocket and pulled out some change. "Get yourself something to eat, please."

"Yeah, I'll do that. Thanks. Times are tough when an ape can't get a decent meal and humans are eating like kings," the chimp said.

Ari turned slowly away. Why can't we apes even take care of our own? she thought bitterly. Why do we put so much energy into capturing humans when so many apes don't have enough to eat or a decent place to sleep? She walked along, lost in thought. Suddenly she bumped up against a looming figure.

"Limbo!" she sputtered, half in surprise and half in joy.

"Limbo," said the homeless chimp, "this a friend of yours?"

Limbo, an orangutan with orange fur that grew in random tufts about his face, eyed the ape. "You might say that, firstly. And secondly you might also say that she's the daughter of a senator, and if he knew she was here, he'd probably have the army burn this whole neighborhood to the ground. So keep your trap shut, got it?" He glanced sideways at the chimp in rags, as if he'd enjoy stepping on her like a bug.

The chimp looked startled at his harsh response. Limbo was not known for his tact or kindness.

Ari turned and looked at Limbo. He was middle-aged, younger than her father but several years older than Attar. He wore a blue coat that had been all the rage last season. It was stained and frayed at the edges.

"Ari, daughter of Sandar," Limbo said, with just the slightest bit of acid in his voice. "What brings you to the heart of my own personal empire?" He spread his long orangutan arms wide to take in the entire run-down street.

"I asked at your old house. They said I'd find you down here," she explained. "How are you?"

The orangutan puffed out his cheeks. "How am I? Oh, fine, fine. Just look where I'm living these days. How could I be anything but fine. I mean, it's not exactly posh, but then I've fallen on hard times since your father decided to make my life miserable!"

Ari straightened her shoulders. "He wasn't after you, Limbo, and you know it. He was trying to reform the fruit traders because they were stealing—"

"It wasn't stealing!" Limbo complained. "It was . . . it was borrowing. That's what it was. The shopkeepers got their money back."

"After you'd used it to buy your own booths at the market to sell fruit for lower prices. You took their money and then put them out of business. My father was doing his job to protect them."

"Well, what about his job to protect me?" Limbo grunted. "I pay taxes, too. Well, I usually pay them anyway. And besides, I helped get him elected."

"After you ran against him for office and called him a straight-laced do-gooder who read too many books and stepped on too many toes."

Limbo tugged at his fur. "He still remembers that?"

"Oh, yeah."

"Well!" Limbo said, "I'm on to bigger and better things, now. A little business deal that will put me back on top, if everything goes the way I've planned it."

Ari felt the fur on her neck stand on end. She knew it—her guess had been right. If the military was turning the human control problem into a slave trade, Limbo was just the kind of ape to make a profit from it. "What kind of business deal?"

Limbo winked at her. "Humans. They're a gold mine. The military lets me hire off-duty soldiers for next to nothing to go out and capture wild humans. I clean them up and then sell them to the priests for ten times the cost!" The orangutan hopped up and down in sheer excitement. "It squashes the fruit game!"

"Really?" Ari asked, pretending to be impressed. She was old enough to know that male apes liked to be impressive. "But humans? Isn't it dangerous?" she said in mock concern.

"Dangerous? You're more likely to get your toes run over by a cart than to get hurt by these humans. Especially when I'm through with them. Would you like to see?"

"Yes," Ari said. "I think I would."

Limbo turned excitedly toward a boarded-up building Ari had just passed, bouncing and chattering like a little ape baby. "Oh, I'm sure you'll be impressed. And you know, if you thought you wanted to mention it to your father, I mean, just to tell him that his old friend Limbo is on the up and up now, and doing work with the government higher-ups themselves, I wouldn't mine. Maybe we could have lunch, or perhaps a dinner at that wonderful house of yours—"

He continued, but Ari stopped listening as they reached the boarded-up door. Without missing a beat, the orangutan pushed the door open ("Just looks boarded up to keep out the riffraff," he explained) and walked inside. Two grim-looking gorillas sat up as the door opened, then eased back into their chairs when they saw it was Limbo. The orangutan nodded at them and led Ari down a long hall that opened up into a big warehouse, its roof reaching up three stories. Instead of being filled with boxes, this warehouse was lined with six large cages. Each cage was filled with humans. Some of the humans were filthy, their hair matted and their bodies covered with animal skins. Others were cleaner, with shaved heads or trimmed hair, and wearing simple robes that had obviously been made by apes.

"A few of these catches have already been cleaned up

and made ready for delivery," Limbo explained as they entered the room. "But most of them are new acquisitions, and they still have to be sanitized. You'd be surprised how hard it is to clean the filth off these things."

As they walked down the central aisle between the cages, Ari looked at the prisoners in horror. They were packed tightly into cages, with barely enough room to stand. Some bowed their heads when she looked at them, while others stared at her with vacant or terrified eyes. A few glared at her hatefully.

Only one human moved. As she past the middle cage, Ari felt something tug at her sleeve. She glanced down and saw a human hand clutching at her arm. Stifling a cry of alarm, she looked up and found herself looking at a pair of bright, clear eyes that burned with a steady light. They were eyes she recognized instantly.

She was looking at Sarai.

"Get your hands off her, you filthy human!" Limbo snapped. He pulled a small, thin crop from his sleeve and slapped it across Sarai's arm. The human shouted and pulled her hand back.

"Sorry about that, my dear," Limbo said soothingly. "But as you see, it's easily corrected. It just takes a firm hand to teach them their place."

Ari's mouth felt dry. She had been horrified at the sight of *any* humans treated so brutally, but Sarai was the one human she knew well. It was Sarai, in fact, who had once saved Ape City from the plague. It was unthinkable that this human could now be imprisoned and beaten by an ape.

"Are they . . . is it . . . " Ari tried to form a sentence. She knew she ought to ask something, to sound interested or intelligent, but her mind was blank.

Limbo, always pleased with the sound of his own voice, filled in the blanks. "Oh, I know what you're thinking. In the past, apes have usually raised domesticated humans as servants. Safer that way, of course. Humans raised in captivity are always easier to manage. But not always available, eh?" Limbo tapped his head to show he'd been using his brain. "The waiting list for human servants is longer than a spider monkey's tail, and it takes years to grow them to an age where they're worth anything. Why hold things up when there are entire herds of them infesting the countryside?"

"Oh, I see," Ari managed to sputter.

"And, of course, the problem would only have gotten worse. Humans have always been trapped in the wild, but never on this scale. The government is using a lot of this stock for its own purposes. A few we'll be able to sell privately. But it was a job that had to be done. And, of course, I was happy to fill the need."

"What . . . " Ari forced herself to think. "You said the government will buy most of them. What are they, um, used for?"

Limbo's answer was interrupted by the sound of several doors flying open, followed by hoots and the cracking of whips. A dozen apes entered, carrying whips or clubs or both. The armed apes moved to each cage that contained uncleaned humans, and, one by one, they opened the cages and drove the prisoners down the aisle toward a door at the far end of the warehouse.

As she watched, Ari saw that the slave drivers were actually working to separate the humans into two groups. One group was made up of the biggest, strongest males. It also included any average-looking males and females who wore crude skins and animal furs. Into the other group, the slavers drove males and females who wore slightly more refined clothes—skins that had been tanned and treated, or primitive jewelry made of leather cords strung with polished stones and shells. Sarai was pushed into this group.

Once the two groups were separated, both were driven out the far door.

Without asking, Ari followed. This door led outside, to a loading area with a raised ramp. Two carts, their beds lined and roofed with iron bars, waited as the two groups of humans were loaded into separate carts. Iron doors clanged, and the carts had started to roll away.

"Uh, well, it was nice to see you, Limbo," Ari said. "Thank you for the tour."

"Oh, any time," Limbo said, wringing his hands. "Be sure to say hello to your father. And no hard feelings about the fruit incident!"

Ari waved over her shoulder and hurried after the cart.

As she followed the carts rattling down the lane, Ari did not know whether to be angry or horrified or both. It was bad enough that apes raised domesticated humans and treated them like cattle—but to pluck humans from their natural habitat and imprison them, that was cruelty in its purest form.

. . . . .

The carts rattled slowly down the muddy lane, running through the warehouse district toward the edge of town. The slave wagons moved slowly, so at first it wasn't hard for Ari to keep up. But after a half hour of following, her feet started to hurt and her legs ached, and she began to wonder just where the humans were being taken.

The carts followed the warehouse district at the lowest level of the slope until it reached the walls, then they turned sharply, heading up the hill toward the top of the city. Ari grunted. It was going to be a long climb.

An hour later, the sun was high in the sky, Ari's fur was matted with sweat, and the cart was approaching the very top of the hill around which the city was built. They had taken the long way up, avoiding several streets that shot directly up to the top. But once they got close, Ari had a sense of their destination. The top of the hill had been leveled by what must have been an immense amount of work. On the wide, flat space, Ari could see the beginning of the new temple that the city was building. The walls were already being raised, with massive stones being piled on top of massive stones to form a gigantic square. There were no civilians around the building site. It was a tradition among apes that no one saw a new temple until it was completely built and blessed by the priests.

But there was a mass of activity around the site. Even though it was only half done, the temple looked impressive. A set of wide stone steps led up to the incredibly thick walls. Ari could already tell that the walls were being built to form a great dome four stories high. Several squads of ape soldiers patrolled the site, and Ari could see gangs of humans hauling stones on wheeled carts, or using pulleys to haul the blocks up atop the walls as ape overseers watched them closely. This surprised Ari—not because humans were being used for manual labor, but because Timon the high priest despised humans so much, it seemed odd that he would let them near the city's main temple.

No one bothered Ari as she watched the carts roll to a stop near the half-built temple. Guards opened the cages, and the humans were herded out, encouraged by jabs and strikes from clubs and whips. At that moment, there was an angry cry from the walls, then more shouts. Suddenly, one of the guards shouted, "Bring the new humans over. Bring them now! They need to see this!"

The guards applied their weapons with even greater enthusiasm, driving the newly captured humans toward the walls. None of them seemed to care about Ari, so she followed them right up to the closest stone stack. Here, a wall had not been finished, but a huge stone block—taller than Attar—was dangling from a net of ropes ready to be lowered into a slot designed for it.

One of the guards jumped up onto the wall. Reaching back down, he hauled up a human by the hair and held the man out to the crowd. Even Ari, who knew quite well how strong gorillas were, was impressed with the guard's ability to hold a full-grown human up with one arm.

"Humans!" the guard shouted. "This human did not do his work. He did not complete his task on time, and another stone is not ready for lifting. He will be punished."

Without another word, the guard turned and tossed the human into the space beneath the hanging stone. "No, no!" he cried.

The guard waved to the ape overseers who were holding the ropes in place. "Lower it!"

The overseers nodded. They released a hook holding the ropes taut. Instantly, the stone's weight dragged it down, slowly lowering it into place. "No, no, n—!" The human's screams echoed for a moment, then fell instantly silent.

"By Semos," Ari whispered. She looked around. The humans who were already working bowed their heads sadly. The new arrivals murmured and seemed on the verge of panic—but with the crack of the whip the guards reminded them to be still.

Ari saw Sarai glance around, her movements calm as she searched for some way to escape. But when she spotted Ari and met her gaze, Ari saw sheer terror in Sarai's eyes.

CHAPTER TWELVE

That Sarai, chief of the tek clan that had come over the mountains, had been caught was a stroke of incredibly bad luck. It was also the kind of dumb accident that did not fit the image of a courageous leader. Sarai had always imagined that if she were ever captured or killed, it would be while she was fighting invincible odds, or after she was caught in the most diabolical plot the apes could hatch. She was the chief of a great clan, and one of the wisest of her people—she deserved a great story.

Her capture was not great. It was hardly even an event. When Birn had burst into camp bearing news of Daena's capture, Sarai had set out almost immediately, taking only a small sack full of provisions. She did not have a specific plan in mind, but she knew she had to find Ari. She also knew that Ari was the daughter of some important chief of the apes, so the human hoped to sneak into the city and mingle with any humans there just long enough to hear where this important chief might live. Then Sarai would go to Ari and ask for help in freeing her daughter. And Ari would do it—Sarai knew that intuitively. Ari was hardly more than a child among the apes—not much older, in ape years, than Daena was to her people—but Sarai had witnessed firsthand how strong and resourceful the young ape could be. Ari was sympathetic, exactly the kind of ape she hoped to befriend. All Sarai had to do was find her.

She didn't even get close. Only two hours away from camp, she had walked right into an ape patrol. They had been as surprised to see her as she was to see them—but there were six of them, and they had reacted fast. Before Sarai knew it, a net was thrown over her head and an ape smashed a club across the back of her neck. She'd woken up hours later, in Limbo's slave pens in the middle of Ape City. For the first time in her life, Sarai had felt crushed. Imprisoned, she could only wonder what had happened to her daughter, and what might happen to her husband and her clan.

And then the miracle happened—Ari had walked into her prison. Sarai had not believed her eyes. The only apes she had seen were the soldiers who'd brought her and the guards who'd beaten them and thrown them scraps of food. Then, the first visitor Sarai saw was the young female chimpanzee. In that moment, Sarai's hopes were lifted out of the depths of her despair, and she knew, beyond all doubt, that there was a way to survive this.

Now, a few minutes after her arrival at the temple, Sarai's confidence was shaken again. She had just seen the poor human crushed beneath the stone. All her fears for her daughter flooded back to her. But she forced herself to remain calm. She would need all her wits about her to survive this.

"Move!" a guard snarled. He cracked a whip over their heads. Sarai's group was quickly hustled toward the wide, high steps that led into the temple itself.

"What is this place?" she asked one of the other humans. "Do you know?"

The other human, a tek from another clan, shook her head. "I heard someone say it is where the apes worship their god. I did not know even apes could build anything as big as this."

At the top was a flat, open plaza that stood before the doors to the temple dome itself. In this plaza, the ape guards cracked their whips again and ordered the humans to drop to their knees.

Sarai and the others obeyed. A moment later, a red-robed figure appeared at the door and glided slowly, elegantly toward them. The ape in red wore a veil across his face, completely hiding his features. One of the ape guards nodded his head. "High Priest Timon, the humans are ready to be addressed."

The veiled head nodded. Without pulling aside his veil, the ape priest stepped toward the small group of humans and began to speak. "Semos has smiled on you, humans. Your worthless lives have been given a purpose. You have been chosen to help us build the greatest Temple of Semos that apekind has ever known." He paused, as though expecting some reaction from the humans. But all of them were either terrified, bewildered, or both. "All the humans brought here will help, but your group has been singled out. While the rest of your kind do manual labor, hauling rocks and so forth, you will be educated."

Sarai perked up. *Educated?*

Timon continued. "You were selected because we have found indications that you, somehow, use more of your puny brains than your brothers."

Suddenly it occurred to Sarai why they had been divided into two groups. She had already noticed that most of the humans in her group were teks. The apes had learned to tell teks from the more primitive wildings, and had decided to put the two groups to different uses.

Timon held out a roll of parchment covered in lines and scratches and symbols. "None of you know what this means," he said. "But you will. These are letters and numbers, and soon you will know enough to be able to read them and use them to help put the stones in place. The service you are doing is holy—you are doing the work of Semos. You allow us to raise our temple from its foundations to its highest tip in half the time it would take if we used apes alone. Semos truly smiles on you."

"But . . . " The ape's voice suddenly grew cold and hard.

"Fail us, and the penalty is death. And not just death for you. Your entire crew will die. And to prove that we are serious, watch."

He raised his hands, and eight more guards appeared in the doorway to the temple, driving a group of eight humans before them. The apes made the eight humans kneel before the new arrivals and bow their heads.

The guard who had first addressed Timon hurried forward and whispered something to the veiled ape. Timon hesitated, then said loud enough for all to hear, "They already witnessed a human being made into an example, did they? So what? These humans have thick skulls. They need more reminders. Kill them anyway."

The priest raised an arm and the eight soldiers raised their swords. One of the humans, a small female, raised her head defiantly, unwilling to cower while the apes killed her. As she did, Sarai saw the human's face. It was her daughter.

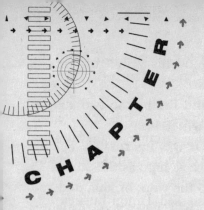

THIRTEEN

Sarai shoved her way past the humans before her and dove at the priest's feet. "Please!" she cried. "Please don't!"

Timon recoiled in surprise, and the apes delayed their strikes, shocked by the boldness of this human. Sarai lay on her stomach, clutching the hem of Timon's robes. Even when a guard rushed forward to pull her away, she would not let go.

"Please, please!" she begged. She had never begged for anything before in her life, but this was no time for pride. "That is my daughter. Please save her life. I'll do anything!"

A second ape pounced on her, prying her fingers from the priest's clothes and dragging her back. "You will not touch the person of the high priest!" the ape snarled.

"Wait," Timon said, smoothing his wrinkled robes. He stepped forward, leaning so close that Sarai could just see the outline of his ape face behind his veil. "You are the mother of one of these creatures?"

Sarai, her arms pinned behind her by the two guards, nodded. "The little one. My daughter. Please."

The veiled face studied her. It was inscrutable. Finally, Timon said, "You will work twice as hard as the others. To save the life of one, you will do the work of four, and you will do it all on time. Or I will have your daughter destroyed."

"Yes. Anything," Sarai replied.

"And you will make sure the little troublemaker herself pulls her load. At the first hint of trouble from her, she will be destroyed."

"Yes," Sarai promised.

Sarai thought she saw the face behind the veil twist into a cruel smile. "Very well."

Timon waved his hand, and the guard holding Daena grabbed her by the hair and dragged her forward. He pushed her back to her knees once she reached Sarai. Mother and daughter looked at each other, and a wordless exchange passed between them. Relief and joy flooded through Sarai, while Daena's eyes filled with tears of fear and love. Sarai broke eye contact and looked up at Timon again. "And the others . . . I recognize them. I am their clan chief. They will listen to me."

Again, Timon sounded interested. "You can make them work harder?"

"Yes."

"Follow orders?"

"Yes."

"And you will see to it they make no trouble, as long as I spare them."

"Yes."

"No." Timon raised his hand and let it fall. Sarai threw an arm over her eyes to block out the sight. But she could still hear the sound. A horrific *whoosh* filled the air as seven swords swung down, followed by the sickening sound of metal on flesh. Some of the new arrivals gasped or screamed. None of the seven humans made a sound—they never had the chance.

Sarai felt a powerful hand in her hair, tilting her chin up, and once again she was staring into the crimson veil. "Wh-why?" she gasped.

The high priest said, "Don't think you're my equal. Negotiating with humans is beneath me. And you are not their clan chief. You are a slave, and you will do what you are told. Those deaths were just a reminder of that. Do not forget it."

Timon let go of her and walked away, his feet, hidden beneath the robes, carrying him across the plaza in a strange, level glide, undisturbed by the fact that he had just had seven humans killed.

"Up!" snarled the chief guard. "To the holding pens!"

The newcomers were rousted and marched across the plaza. They walked parallel to the doors until they reached the corner of the building, then turned to the side of the flat hilltop, where several large pens had been erected.

As they walked, Sarai and Daena inched closer to each other until they were near enough to be heard at a whisper. Daena spoke first, her voice hardly more than a sob. "Mama."

The sound nearly brought tears to Sarai's eyes. Daena hadn't called her that in years. "Are you all right? Have they hurt you?"

"No," the girl said. "I mean, no more than anyone else. Is the clan . . . ? How did you . . . ?"

"I came to get you," Sarai said, realizing how ridiculous that sounded.

"Oh, Mother, I'm so sorry!" Daena said, her voice quavering. "You're here because of me. I didn't mean to get caught. It was so stupid. Pak got caught, too. Is Birn all right?"

"He made it back to the clan. I came as soon as he told me. I . . . I was pretty half-witted myself." Sarai reached out just enough to brush her hand against her daughter's. Their fingers intertwined. Sarai managed a smile. "Between us I figure we've got one full brain. Let's use it to get out of here."

"How? You saw what they do to anyone who causes trouble. And there are guards everywhere."

"We'll find a way," Sarai insisted. "Remember, apes aren't smarter than us, they just know more. There's always a way. We'll find it."

Their group reached the holding pens. "New slaves, into

this pen! You there!" The soldier jabbed the handle of his whip into Daena's stomach. "You, over here. You're being assigned a new crew, now that your old one's lost its head!" The joke made him laugh a harsh, barking laugh. Daena threw her mother one last glance, then followed the ape to another part of the compound.

Sarai followed the crowd of humans into the holding pen. Even as guards closed the cage door and locked it, she did not lose hope. Her daughter was alive, and Ari knew where she was. A feeling of certainty warmed the edges of her mind—almost like a sense of purpose. Sarai had the distinct feeling that everything was going exactly as it was supposed to.

Stupid, she told herself. You're turning your hopes into delusions.

"Humans, listen closely!"

The guard's harsh voice snapped Sarai to attention. There were twenty others crammed into the holding pen with her, and every one of them straightened up obediently. None of them wanted to end up under the apes' swords— or worse, under the stones.

"Tomorrow your new life begins," the guard said. "Consider yourselves lucky. You will not be sent to the quarry to break stones and shape blocks. You will not be put on the dragging crews that bring the stones up to the hilltop. You have been chosen as masons. You will learn how to lay the stones properly in their places, using this."

The ape held up a roll of parchment, letting it unravel to

reveal a long string of numbers and letters. Sarai, like all humans, did not know how to read. But she understood what writing was.

"You will learn to read these symbols. You will know what they mean, and they will tell you where to put the stones. If you fail, the stones will be put on you." He held up another scroll. On this one, the delicate string of symbols had been replaced by one crude drawing—a human being crushed by a stone. "You had better learn fast what one of these means, or you'll certainly learn the meaning of the other."

As Sarai listened, she could hardly believe her ears. The apes were going to teach her to read and write. They were going to teach her how to use symbols to build buildings. Her own words echoed in her head. Apes aren't smarter than us, they just know more.

Now they were going to teach her what they knew.

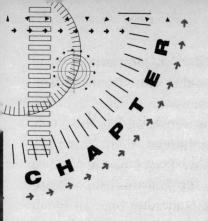

CHAPTER

FOURTEEN

Night fell, drawing Sarai's first day of captivity to a close. The apes hadn't bothered much with their group—whatever plan they had for this particular pen, it must begin tomorrow. Only once did a guard stop by, pouring scraps of food into a small trough at one end of the enclosure. Otherwise, they were ignored. As the light receded, work crews were marched back to other empty pens and locked away for the night. Sarai tried to catch a glimpse of Daena, but there were more than a hundred humans in different work gangs, and her daughter was lost among them.

After sunset, guards roamed the hilltop in groups of two or four, sometimes ignoring the human pens completely, sometimes rattling the cage doors to check the locks. A single fire burned in the center of the compound, its light barely bright enough to reach the pens. The hilltop grew cold, and the humans huddled close for warmth. Sarai didn't know any of the others—they were from clans on the far side of the plains. But they were all teks, and Sarai was glad to learn that their clans were similar to hers. Teks were learners. They believed that humans could master ape ways, and tried to create their own. If such people could be kept alive, and be given a place to flourish, Sarai believed that they could pull humans up and away from an age of stones and wooden spears to an age of iron and steel.

Another prisoner, a woman dressed in one long piece of carefully cut animal hide and a necklace made of river stones, shifted over until she was sitting beside Sarai. "That was a brave thing you did."

Sarai accepted the compliment with a nod. "I was just desperate. That was my daughter."

"You must be a good chief," the woman said. "My name is Pica."

They shook hands. "I'm Sarai."

"Sarai. Our chief was killed in the ape raid. I hope when we have a new one, he is as strong as you are."

Sarai replied, "If we escape, your clan can join ours."

Pica scoffed. "And if my grandsire had fur, he'd be an ape." She shook her head. "You are dreaming."

Sarai nodded. "Yes, I am. But some dreams come true. You never know what will happen next."

As Sarai spoke, a figure appeared through the darkness, moving toward their cage. The figure's face was hidden beneath the folds of a long brown cloak, and it carried a small lamp in its hand. The lamp's flame burned just bright enough to reveal the newcomer's face.

"Sarai," said Ari, her voice a frightened whisper. "I'm looking for Sarai."

"Ari." Sarai gingerly moved among the cramped prisoners until she found a space against the bars. "Ari." She said the name again as if it were the answer to a prayer.

"I . . . I shouldn't be here," Ari said quietly. She shifted back and forth from foot to foot, a movement Sarai was learning meant nervousness. "I'm a senator's daughter, so I was able to tell a guard I had a reason, but . . ." Her voice trailed off. It took her a moment to find it again. "It's dangerous for me to be here. But I couldn't sit at home, knowing you were here."

Sarai felt eyes on her back and knew that the other prisoners were staring at them. But she didn't have time to explain.

"Thank you," Sarai whispered. "Thank you for coming. Is there . . . is there anything you can do for us?"

"I don't know. Maybe I could sneak you out of the city. I know a way. But you'd have to get out of here, away from the guards and the temple. I don't know how to do that." Ari reached through the bars and put a hand on Sarai's wrist. "I want to help you. I saw what happened to that poor human today. I . . . I'm ashamed of my species. You must hate us."

Sarai shook her head. "I can't let myself hate you. If I hate you, then I'll fall into the same trap as all my people.

I'll want to fight and kill apes, and if we do that, we humans will lose. I still want to find a way to show apes that humans are intelligent and should be treated with respect."

Ari patted the human's hand. "That is a curious thing. From what I've seen, your worst enemies are doing that for you." She explained. "The two most powerful human haters in the government are Colonel Thade and Timon the high priest. But they seem to be the ones behind this latest plan to capture wild humans and domesticate them to work on this project. The more they do that, the more apes will see that humans can be taught."

Sarai understood her meaning. "Especially when this temple is done. Humans will have helped build it. And there will be humans in the city with knowledge given by the apes. You might be on to something, Ari."

The young ape nodded. "As long as you can stay alive long enough to see it through."

The human shivered. "I'll do my best."

A guard carrying a torch passed by, his armor clinking as he walked. He grunted at Ari as he did, and she nodded. "I have to go," she whispered. "I think my favor is about over. Is there anything I can do for you? I hate to see you locked up like this after what you did for us."

"Is there a way out of the city?" Sarai asked.

The young ape considered. "I think so. There's an old way that I know. My friends and I used to play in the water channels when I was a little younger. There's an old tunnel that leads under the wall. I could show it to you—but I can't get you out of here."

Sarai nodded. "I don't want to leave just yet. Especially if I can gain knowledge for my people. Ari, will you come again?"

The chimpanzee nodded. "Yes, as soon as I can."

Ari pulled her hood tighter about her face, stood, and hurried off into the darkness.

The woman, Pica, inched up next to Sarai. "What's that all about?" she asked.

Sarai sighed. "With any luck, it's the beginning of a new age for apes and humans." Then, exhausted, she lay herself down on the hard ground and slept.

Sarai thought she had slept for only a few minutes before she was rudely awakened by an elbow in her ribs. Her eyes flew open and she propped herself up on her hands, blinking. Gray light filled the sky as the sun lifted itself slowly over the horizon. Sarai shook the drowsiness from her head and forced herself to stand. Around her, the others were rousing themselves, too. Several apes had surrounded the cage and were banging on the bars. "Wake up! Up, you hairless brutes! Up!"

The cage door flew open and two or three apes waded in among the humans, kicking and shoving those who hadn't already gotten to their feet.

Once the prisoners were awake, the apes marched them single file out of the holding pen and over to a large tent that had been set up along the base of the growing temple wall. Inside, they were ordered to sit on the ground in front of a large plank of wood. Several pieces of parchment had been pinned to the surface of the wood. As soon as the humans were settled in their places, with guards barking warnings at them, a small, wizened baboon entered the tent and tottered near the front. Behind him followed a human. Sarai instantly recognized him as a member of her own clan. It was Mad Luc!

The human followed the baboon right up to the front of the room, then faded off to one side as the ape spoke. "My name is Professor Ganji. My job is impossible, but I've been ordered to try it anyway. You have all been chosen because you supposedly use more than your normal share of brainpower. I find that hard to believe in a human, but orders are orders." The ape sighed as though a worldly burden had been laid on his shoulders. "You will be taught to read a basic diagram. Do any of you know what a diagram is?"

None of the humans responded. Professor Ganji slapped his head several times. "Come, come. No one knows a diagram? How about a picture? Can anyone here draw a picture?"

A tiny ripple, a sort of stifled reaction, rolled through the small group. Most tek clans drew pictures. High in the mountains was a cave where tek picture makers, after a long hike and a difficult crawl through the narrow tunnels, came to a wide cavern, where they would paint pictures on the walls. But it was a secret place, sacred to the human clans, and none of the teks wanted to reveal it to the apes.

"Oh, by Semos!" the baboon snapped. "You creatures must know something. Look at this human." Professor Ganji pointed at Mad Luc, who kept his eyes on the floor. "For a creature with such a small brain, he grasped the knowledge quite quickly."

The other teks glared at Luc disapprovingly as Ganji continued. "You will either learn what we have to teach you, or you'll be sent down to the brute pens with the rest of the humans. They don't need to understand anything. They work until they can no longer lift stones. Then they are left to die. It's all the same to me." Ganji turned to Mad Luc. "You, teach them. If they have not learned to read a basic diagram, to count out measurements, by the end of the day, they and you will be put beneath a stone."

With that, the baboon turned and trotted out of the tent.

As soon as he was gone, Pica, the woman Sarai had met, spoke up. "You! How could you be helping these—"

"Sh!" Sarai hissed for the woman to be quiet. She pointed toward one of the sides of the tent, where the silhouette of an ape guard could be seen. There were several of them posted around the outside of the pavilion. She waited for them to retreat before she spoke. "We have better things to do than argue."

Mad Luc looked up, recognizing Sarai's voice and spotting her. His face lit up. "Sarai! I'm so glad to see you. I mean, not here, but you know—"

"You're not my chief yet," Pica said to Sarai. "This man helps apes!"

"I know him," said another. "My brother trades with his clan. His own people say he's mad."

Sarai moved forward until she was standing next to Luc. "I am his chief, and I say he is not. He sees what others do not. He thinks of things that others don't think of. And by learning what the apes know, he is following my orders."

The humans looked at Sarai in shock . . . and none of them was more surprised than Luc himself. Without missing a beat, Sarai continued. "I am clan leader of the teks from across the mountains. I have a plan to build a safe place for humans to live. But to do it, we need knowledge the apes have. That's why Luc and I are here." She looked at Mad Luc for confirmation. The confused man just nodded his head, bewildered but willing to be led. "Once we learn what we need to know, we'll all be able to escape."

"Ridiculous," said another tek whom Sarai did not recognize.

"No," Pica said. "Remember last night. An ape came to visit her at the pens."

"Maybe she does have a plan," a third human said.

"I do," Sarai said firmly. "If you'll all follow my lead, we'll get out of here. But until it's time to escape, we must learn as much as the apes will teach us."

The teks hesitated, but then they began to murmur their assent.

"Good," Sarai nodded. She turned to Luc. "Then we should begin the lesson."

Mad Luc nodded. "Absolutely." Then he lowered his voice. "Excuse me, Sarai. But what, exactly, is this plan of yours?"

Sarai allowed herself only the tiniest moment of doubt. "I don't know yet."

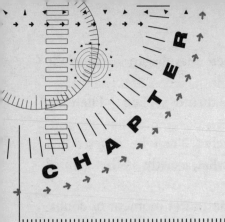
FIFTEEN

The next three days were Sarai's greatest dream and her worst nightmare. For three days she and the other humans sat in the tent and learned. They learned how to read the ape symbols for measuring short distances. "Millimeter." "Centimeter." "Meter." They learned about a simple machine called a "pulley." Sarai was amazed when, using a pulley and a rope, she was able to lift three other humans off the ground all by herself. They learned about how to make an "arch"—which was simply a way to pile stones together so that they pushed against one another instead of falling down.

Sarai also learned the ingenious method the apes had developed for laying stones one atop another. The stones they used were cut with deep grooves in them. Ropes were then tied around the stone, running through the grooves.

These ropes were then used to haul the stones up on the pulleys. The pulleys were moved into position and the stones were lowered into place, ropes and all. Then the ropes were simply pulled free, sliding through the grooves like a sword sliding out of a scabbard.

And with every new thing they learned, Sarai's belief proved to be true: Apes were not smarter than humans. The teks grasped every single piece of knowledge, swallowing it hungrily, making it part of their own lore. Sarai could not have asked for a better education if she had marched into the ape Senate and demanded it.

But that knowledge came with a price. The apes never let their captives forget that they were slaves. Ape guards were everywhere. During every moment when they were not learning, the humans were locked in their pens. Twice in three days, for no apparent reason, soldiers stormed into the tent, picked a human at random, and dragged him away. They never saw those two humans again.

"What did they do?" Pica asked. "Why were they punished?"

"I don't know," Sarai said.

Luc answered. "They didn't do anything. The soldiers just pick people at random and drag them off. To make a point to the rest of us."

Sarai wasn't afraid only for herself. For three days she had not seen her daughter. And for three days she feared for her clan. She knew Karubi could hold them together, but Vasich was surely causing trouble. He might even find a way to take control of the clan, and then he was bound to lead them to one disaster or another.

On the morning of the fourth day of Sarai's captivity, they were roused by the guards banging on the bars of their pen. But as they stumbled out of the cage, they were not led to the learning tent as usual. They were quickly divided into small gangs of two or three. Sarai was coupled with Luc, and together they were led over to one section of the temple. Bands of humans were already busy hauling a great stone block—a block that weighed as much as a hundred men—up to the wall. The block was resting on wooden logs that acted as rollers, and thick ropes had been attached to the block. Forty humans pulled on the rope, while a group of four worked around the block itself. Each time the giant block passed one of the rollers, the small gang snatched it up and ran to the front of the block and laid it down again. Sarai was pleased to see two familiar faces working the rollers. Daena and Pak, always quick on their feet, had been assigned to work in her gang. They both nodded to her, and Daena even managed a smile as they sprinted to get ahead of the slow-moving block.

An ape waved them over. He wasn't wearing armor, so Sarai knew he was not a soldier. She guessed that he was one of the builders of the temple. "You there," he barked. "This stone is yours. Put it in this spot here. If the stone doesn't go on the right spot, the stone will go on you. Understand?" He shoved a piece of parchment into Luc's hands and walked away.

Luc opened the parchment and Sarai studied it over his shoulder. "Can we do this?" she wondered.

Luc nodded. "Don't worry. I did five or six before they asked me to teach you. It's not hard. In fact, I was able to—"

He clamped his mouth shut as a band of apes marched by. Sarai recognized the red-robed priest Timon. Beside him walked an important-looking chimpanzee with a fierce look in his eyes. Behind them walked another armored gorilla— and this one Sarai recognized. She stared at him until he felt her eyes on him and turned to look.

Attar.

Sarai raised her hand in a small gesture. Attar saw it but did not respond.

The group of apes stopped near where they worked and surveyed the temple wall. "I have to admit," Timon was saying, "the work is progressing much faster now that we've allowed the humans to supervise their own work. There just weren't enough architects to watch every little bit of masonry."

The chimpanzee grunted. "Parrots repeating what they hear, that's all. Dogs trained to fetch. How is the interior coming? When will it be done?"

"We're estimating only a few more days. . . ." Timon was saying as they moved off.

The third ape, Attar, hesitated. The other two didn't seem to need him, so he turned back and stared at Sarai again. Tentatively, she took a step forward. He did not growl at her, so she took another step, and then walked up to him. He was even bigger than she remembered, and his face had hardened into the angry gorilla mask she'd seen on other ape soldiers.

"You . . . you remember who I am?" she asked.

"I remember," Attar growled, his voice a low rumble of thunder in his throat.

"You might have said hello," Sarai said, "considering I saved your life."

Attar's scowl deepened. "Be grateful I don't look more excited. If Colonel Thade knew who you were, he would cut you down where you stand."

"Why?"

"He believes you tried to poison my mind. You tried to make me believe apes and humans were equal."

Sarai shook her head. "I didn't do anything except keep you alive. You owe me a favor for that."

The big gorilla sneered. "You did not keep me alive. It was the will of Semos that I lived. Just as it is the will of Semos that you are here. Do you know who Semos is?"

Sarai shrugged. "Your ape god."

"He is the only deity!" Attar growled. "Semos is the First Ape. The divine brought down into the being of a mortal ape. He saved me from the plague. And now you are here to build his temple. You ask for a favor? There is no greater reward than serving Semos."

"And being held prisoner?" Sarai said. "Being put under stones?"

"Only the disobedient are punished," Attar replied gruffly.

"Attar, front and center!" the fierce chimp called. "We're inspecting the interior!"

"Yes, sir!" He turned to go. Sarai felt her moment slipping away. Daringly she reached out and touched his thick, muscled arm. Attar whirled back at her and snorted angrily. Sarai felt her stomach drop away and her knees went weak, but she held her ground. He was no different than Vasich, she told herself. He was strong, but strength wasn't everything.

"I saved your life," she said, meeting his fierce look with her own clear, steady gaze. "You'll remember that some day."

And then, risking his anger, she turned her back on him and walked away.

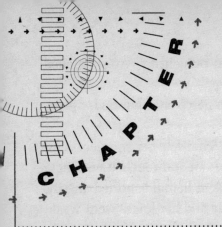

SIXTEEN

It was not forbidden to enter an unfinished temple, but it was discouraged. According to ape beliefs, the spirit of Semos came into a temple only once the priests had blessed it—before that moment, it was an unholy place.

Ari didn't care. On the same morning that Attar encountered Sarai, she was walking up the broad new steps of the growing temple. As she passed through the doors, a lower-level priest—marked by his red robes with the white stripe of a novice down the front—hurried toward her, trying to shoo her out.

"There is no worshiping here!" he said, flapping his hands at her. "Go, go!"

Ari stood her ground. She'd broken rules before—serious ones, made by serious apes in positions of command. She wasn't going to worry much about a little priest barely out of his training. "I'm not here to pray," she said. "I'm an architecture student. I'm here to study."

With that, she passed him by and walked in.

The Temple of Semos was huge. There was no ceiling yet, but she could see from the way the walls rose that the dome would rise two or three hundred feet over her head. At the far end, the altar was nearly complete, with only a few ape masons putting the finishing touches on the stone dais and a little chapel where the statue of Semos itself would rest. She could see humans on the walls all around her, but no humans were allowed here, in the center of the temple.

Beyond the altar, she saw a wall rising up, and atop the wall, she saw a figure that looked familiar to her. Drawing closer, she saw Sarai and another human standing atop one huge stone block as a gang of humans worked to lower another block into place. Sarai looked as if she were in charge. Somehow this didn't surprise Ari. There was a quality about the human female—a sense of strength. She was a leader.

Nearer to the wall, Ari could see that Sarai's group seemed to be working on a small room. The room was right behind the altar, but it didn't lead anywhere. It was almost like a storeroom between the altar and the outer wall.

"Impressive, isn't it?"

Ari jumped into the air, scampering a few feet away as soon as her feet touched the ground.

Colonel Thade had spoken right into her ear. He had a way of sneaking up on people that unnerved them, which was certainly his intent. It's his way of gaining the upper hand, she thought. Making an entrance.

Thade and Timon stood side by side. She didn't know how long they had been standing behind her.

Ari gathered her wits about her. "It is a lot of work, in my opinion, for a superstition."

"Blasphemy!" Timon the priest said.

Thade only looked amused. "You are a young rebel, aren't you?" he said smoothly. "I like that. Don't obey authority blindly. Do your own thinking."

Ari took a few steps closer—not because she wanted to be near Thade, but because she wanted to show him she wasn't afraid. "That's an unusual concept for a military ape, isn't it?"

Thade grinned. "Oh, there are rules to follow . . . for most of us. But you hate that, don't you? You don't like to follow rules. You find them too constricting. They squeeze you." Thade turned to Timon. "You see, Timon, that's all it is. It's not that she doesn't believe in Semos, or that she really likes humans. She just wants to break the rules. It's her youth."

Timon shrugged. "You may be right, Colonel. As long as she remains only her father's problem, it's no concern of mine."

Thade, however, was not so eager to disregard the female chimp. He kept his fierce gaze on her as he said,

"What you need to learn, Ari, is that the squeezing, that pressure, pushes some of us to the top. To the very top."

Ari smirked. "I can't help but notice, Colonel Thade, that the pressure has lifted you only to second place. Behind General Krull."

Thade's lips curled into a snarl, but he calmed himself and said, "For the moment. But my time will come soon. And when it does, you'll be a little older, and a little wiser, and I think you and I shall talk again."

Ari felt like she was getting her feet underneath her again. Thade was intimidating, but part of his power lay in the threat of physical violence. She kept telling herself that he would never harm a senator's daughter. That gave her an advantage. She said confidently, "I think, by that time, I'll be proven right, Colonel. You are actually proving my point here. You are teaching all these humans skills that they'll still have when the temple is complete. Then everyone in Ape City will know what humans are capable of."

Timon laughed out loud. Thade chuckled. "Will they? What exactly will they see?"

The female chimp felt her confidence start to drain away. "Well, naturally, they'll see the humans . . . "

Ari's blood ran cold. The grin on Thade's face widened. His face was smiling, but his eyes remained icy cold and cruel. She thought of the human who had been crushed beneath the stone, and she understood. No ape would ever meet these educated humans. No citizen of Ape City would ever learn how easily the humans learned to become architects. They would all disappear. They were humans from the wild, and no one would ever miss them. Ari shuddered. She had to warn Sarai.

Sarai and Luc stood at the top of the wall and surveyed their work. They had managed to place four huge stone blocks in less than a day. In the excitement of the work, Sarai had forgotten that she was working for apes. The stone blocks had become *her* blocks, the wall was now *her* wall. She watched over her work gang, urging them on. Daena and Pak worked tirelessly—when they weren't moving rollers, they would grab hold of one of the ropes and help the haulers pull.

In her own mind, Sarai was not seeing an ape temple rise before her. She was seeing a human city. Human towers, human walls. Cobblestone streets down which humans could walk in safety. Her own people living like apes. It was the vision she had been searching for.

"We can do this, Luc," she said to the other human. She had known Mad Luc her whole life, of course—her entire clan had grown up together. But no one had paid much attention to the strange man. He rarely spoke to others, and when he did, it was impossible to understand what he was talking about. He could never keep a conversation on track. He would interrupt himself, or change subjects without warning, and he was always, always off by himself tinkering with pieces of wood or strips of leather. Her clan had called this madness. Sarai had recognized it as genius.

For his part, Luc had lost some of his oddness in captivity. It might have been because the threat of death made him focus. Or it might have been because the apes' attempt to educate the humans had caught his interest.

"Yes, we can. There are still things I would like to learn from them. The tools they use to cut stones. And I don't know how they plan to make the big dome overhead. That takes some planning I haven't seen. But I think they will teach us. But, Sarai"—he turned to look at her—"people are dying. Several have died since you arrived, and I saw more killed before. We are paying a price for this knowledge you want."

Sarai flinched. She knew Luc was right. Her people had paid a price for living so close to Ape City. Now they were paying a price for their learning. She knew it had to end. But she also knew that without knowledge more and more of her people would dwindle down to the level of wildings. They would become what the apes thought they were: animals.

The woman looked down from the wall, where her own daughter was working. She did not want Daena in danger. She was a strong leader, but she was also a mother, and she could only hold back her mother's instincts for so long. "You're right, Luc. But how do we escape?"

"You have to do it soon," said a voice behind them. They turned to find Ari climbing up the wall. The chimpanzee vaulted herself easily up to the top and hurried over to Sarai. "You have to leave."

"What's wrong?" Sarai asked.

"I don't know," Ari admitted. "But Thade is not going to let any humans live after this temple is built. I can promise you that. You have to get out of here soon."

Luc looked inward, across the interior of the temple. "If that's true, we have to leave now. Apes don't let us work on the inside of the temple. But when the walls are complete, only the dome will be left. And that means working inside. They won't use humans for that."

Sarai felt a new sense of urgency twist her stomach into a knot. She should have known. This is what a leader should prepare for. In her eagerness to learn from the apes, she hadn't thought of their plans for the humans. She had assumed from the beginning that once this project was done, the apes would start them on some new work. She had never considered that they would be . . . disposed of. But she should have.

She'd thought of herself as a capable leader—far more clever than someone like Vasich. But perhaps she was too clever for her own good.

Desperately, she turned to Ari. "Can you help us?"

From the top of the wall, they could see the landscape all around them. Human work gangs crawled on and below the walls, dragging stone blocks up to the tops. Apes in twos and threes moved among them, checking the placements, and now and then referring to their drawings. Among them all, and circling the outside of the plateau, were ape soldiers in their dark armor.

"I . . . I can show you a way that leads out of the city," Ari said. "Look down there, partway down the hill. Do you see that tree, the big one with the yellow leaves? If you can be there tomorrow night, I will show you a way out."

Sarai studied the tree, memorizing its location, trying to imagine finding it in the dark. "We'll be there."

"But I don't see how you can," Ari replied. "Even if you could get out of your pens, the soldiers would be on you in a moment. You'd never outrun them."

Sarai knew she was right. At their best, humans could not outrun apes in the open. And neither she nor her people were healthy—all were underfed and exhausted from backbreaking labor. "Then . . . there's no way to do it," she whispered.

"Not unless we can escape without the apes *thinking* we escaped," Luc said.

Sarai frowned. "We need a real idea, not just philosophy."

Luc shrugged. "I was being serious."

"What," she asked, "did you have in mind?"

Luc smiled.

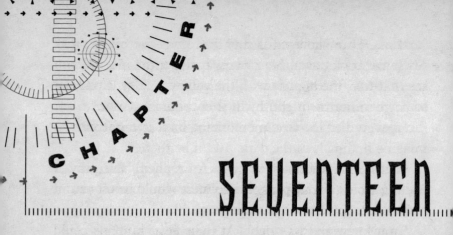

CHAPTER SEVENTEEN

That night, Sarai slept fitfully. Luc had not explained his plan. He said only, "Trust me," and gone off to work with another human crew. The apes had not stopped him—they had long since recognized that he understood their designs and had a way of showing other humans how to work, and they let him move about so long as he got results.

That night, in the pens, he still refused to give details. He had whispered only that, "Voices carry here, even whispers, and I wouldn't want anyone to give away my surprise."

Sarai did not like surprises. Very few surprises were good, and the bad ones were usually worse than anyone thought possible. She spent the night staring up at the barred ceiling of the holding pen. Her thoughts drifted often to Karubi and her clan, waiting somewhere out in the darkness. She wondered if they had given up on her yet. They might already have picked a new chief. For all she knew, they might already have moved. They could be somewhere north or south, in deeper forest, farther from the apes, or they could have retreated back over the mountains.

Maybe, she thought, it's better for them this way. I wanted too much for them. I was willing to lose too many battles to try and win the war.

"Hey," whispered a voice next to her.

Sarai rolled over to find herself looking into the face of Pica, who had curled up next to her and had been watching her stare upward.

"Yes?"

"You're awake, aren't you?"

"I can't sleep," Sarai said. "As exhausted as I am, I can't sleep."

"Me neither," Pica said. "I wanted to tell you something. It's going to sound stupid."

"If you knew how many stupid things I've said and done, you wouldn't be embarrassed to tell me yours."

Pica laughed quietly. "Well, do you remember your first day, when you gave that little speech about a way for humans to use the knowledge apes gave us. I thought you were an idiot when you said that. So did a lot of the rest of us here."

"You might have been right," Sarai admitted.

The other woman shook her head. "I can't say. I think

we've all reached the end of our run, and there isn't much to look forward to but the darkness. Even so . . . " Pica hesitated, looking for words. "Even so . . . this meant something to me in a weird way. You know, I always had the feeling that apes weren't smarter. I always thought if I could just take some time, figure things out, I could do what they did. And this . . . building this thing, even if it is for apes . . . building it has made me feel like I can do things. More than just hunt and tan skins. We can be like apes."

Sarai felt her heart lighten. "We can be better."

With that, she rolled over and fell asleep.

The next day began as every other had begun—with the apes banging on their cage doors. As exhausted as they were, the humans were excited. They knew the walls of the temple were nearly done, and they couldn't help but share in the sense of completion. They practically hurried to their work assignments, hauling the last of the stone blocks up to the top levels.

Sarai and Luc directed their gang to finish the spot just behind the altar. It was the trickiest part of the wall, because a small room had been designed there. Sarai had been curious about that room from the beginning, since it seemed to have no doors, and no halls led to it. It was just an open space between rows of stone blocks. An ape architect instructed Luc and her to lug a medium-size block into position at one end of the room, a block that would seal the room up completely. Working with practiced skill, the human gang dragged the block toward its position, Daena and Pak, as usual, relaying the rollers from back to front.

The block reached the wall. The humans quickly untied the straps lashed to the front of the stone and tied new straps to the top. Then they climbed up to thick tree trunks that were used as levers and began to raise the stone up.

Suddenly, Luc turned to Sarai. "Wish me luck," he said.

"What?"

But Luc was gone. Sarai could hardly believe her eyes when she saw him sprinting away from the wall, across the flat hilltop and toward open ground.

It took a moment for the guards to react. When they did, they were brutal. Horns blew, and apes howled. Several of them sprang on Luc from different directions, driving him into the ground and slapping him several times.

He hadn't gotten more than thirty yards.

One of the gorillas grasped Luc's wrist and dragged him back to the wall, with several soldiers marching in step behind. As they returned to their starting positions, Timon appeared in a swirl of red.

"What is the disturbance?" he demanded impatiently.

"This," the soldier said, lifting Luc by the wrist as though he were rag doll. "It tried to escape."

"Really!" Timon said. He drew back his veil, revealing a pinched, unhappy face, and sniffed at Luc. "Of all the humans, I thought you might actually have some measure of intelligence. Pity." The high priest glanced at the stone suspended in midair. "Put him underneath it," Timon said simply. Then he turned away.

"Luc, no!" Sarai shouted.

"Don't worry!" Luc called back. The apes tossed him beneath the stone. Luc landed on his back, lying on the stone that had been placed before. A panicked look filled his eyes as the ape soldiers waved at the humans manning the giant levers. "Lower it!" one snarled.

The humans hesitated until one ape raised a whip threateningly. Then they bowed their heads and began to lower the stone into place.

"No!" Luc howled. "No!"

The stone dropped lower, and the human reached up, pressing his palms against it as though he could hold it off with his bare hands. The stone continued to descend, and all the humans lost sight of him beneath it. Sarai turned her eyes away. A second later the screaming stopped, and there was a short grinding sound as the stone settled into place atop the stone beneath . . . with Luc crushed between them.

"M-Mother!" Daena whispered. "Why did he—?"

"I don't know," Sarai answered. "I . . . I really don't know."

"Back to work!" the guard shouted. "All of you, back to work!"

Sarai felt all her hopes crushed along with Luc beneath the stones. What had his plan been? Why hadn't he told her? Not, she suddenly realized, that it would have mattered. Any plan that involved sprinting away from the apes was doomed to fail anyway. Maybe Luc had been mad after all. Maybe his genius went only as far as his eyes and hands and their ability to make things. Dealing with the apes might have—it must have—been beyond him.

A whip cracked inches from Sarai's ear, warning her not to loiter. She forced herself to move, as she and her gang went back to the bottom of the wall. There they found three stones waiting to be hauled up, and all around them were other work gangs, entire crowds of them.

"What's going on?" she asked a human she hadn't met.

The human, a man with straight brown hair and a back bowed by hard work, said, "These are the last three stones. Our gangs are done. The apes told us to wait here."

Sarai's crew and two others were told to haul the stones up to their places near the top of the wall. After more than two weeks of this work, they moved quickly, and in less than two hours the stones were at the top. Sarai spent the entire time looking around anxiously, wondering what would happen when they were done. Would they be carted off to be slaughtered? Killed where they stood?

But Sarai saw no hints of the apes' plans. No extra soldiers were gathering on the hilltop. No prison carts rolled up the road. By the time Sarai and the other work gangs had dragged their stones to the top of the wall and raised them with the levers, all was still and calm around the temple. For a moment there was no sound except the creaking of the ropes that held the blocks suspended in air.

These were the last three stone blocks that made up the strange room behind the altar. Checking the diagrams she'd been taught to read, Sarai could tell that these were capstones—each one stretched across the two walls that made the top of the room. When they were in place, the strange space beneath would be sealed.

The humans operating the levers waited for her signal. Sarai nodded. "Put them in place."

"Wait!"

Colonel Thade leaped to the top of the wall. Humans and apes alike gave way before him, scattering like fish before a prowling shark. Behind him came Timon, Attar, and two other soldiers. Not enough to cause concern, but enough to back up any orders the colonel gave.

Thade sniffed the air, wrinkling his nose at the smell of humans in the air. He studied the wall, the empty space beneath them, and the three stones hovering, waiting to be lowered into place.

"These are the last of the stones?" he said.

Timon nodded, and several of the ape architects also wagged their heads vigorously. "Good," Thade said. "Bring all the humans up. I would like a word with them."

In moments, ape soldiers herded all the other work gangs up ramps to the top of the wall. Sarai had never seen all the human prisoners gathered together before. They had always been scattered into work crews, and at night they were held in pens placed all around the temple grounds.

Gathered together now, they made a small battalion of sixty. Anxious as she was, Sarai couldn't help but note their numbers with pride. A mere sixty humans had accomplished so much.

As if to echo her feelings, Thade said in a loud voice, "The work of this temple is not complete, but it has been well begun." The humans murmured, surprised. They'd never heard kind words from an ape—certainly not from a soldier. "The base of the temple has been laid, and the walls are now straight and strong. The dome will be easy to build with such a firm foundation." Thade scanned the crowd of humans, his eyes narrowing, piercing. They stopped briefly on Sarai, singling her out, though she did nothing to attract attention. Then Thade moved on, until he'd surveyed each of his prisoners. "Frankly, no one in Ape City would have thought such a thing possible, for humans to be so well trained. They would be most impressed."

The humans murmured again, astonished—so astonished, in fact, that most of them did not hear Thade's final words: "Pity they will never know. Put them in."

And on that simple order, the ape soldiers converged, shoving humans down into the gap. The first few to go down fell soundlessly, utterly surprised. Then the entire crew screamed, pushing away from the edge, but the apes were too strong. Gorillas scooped up humans in two and threes and tossed them down into the darkness. Sarai turned away from the gap just in time to see a massive gorilla rise up in front of her. The ape snarled and shoved her with immense strength, knocking the breath from her lungs. Sarai had the vague sensation of flying through the air, then she dropped the height of three tall stones and hit the ground hard. She gasped, trying to fill her lungs, and opened her eyes just in time to see bodies falling down on her. She rolled out of the way as someone hit the ground right where she'd lain. Screams filled the small space.

"Get away from the middle!" Sarai shouted over the noise. "Move or you'll be hit!"

Some people listened; some didn't. More bodies tumbled into the pit, until there was no room to go anywhere. Sarai felt herself pressed up against the wall of the temple as the humans in the pit tried to avoid those falling after them. It was a nightmare, and it grew only more terrifying when the bodies stopped falling. Sixty humans had been pushed into a space barely large enough to hold them. They were pressed together like peas in a pod. Some of the prisoners had broken arms or legs in the fall, and they were standing only because the press of bodies kept them upright.

Sarai looked up. She could see the blue sky, turning indigo now in the late afternoon, around the edges of the stone blocks. No apes appeared at the edge of the ledge to look at them. There were no final words. A few seconds after the last human had been dumped into the space, the first stone was lowered. It settled into place with the grating sound that had become so familiar to Sarai. Then the second stone was lowered, plunging most of the gap into darkness.

"No, please!" some of the humans shouted.

"Have mercy on us!" cried others.

Sarai did not yell. She knew the apes would show no mercy. All she could do was choke back tears of frustration. She'd been so stupid. This had been their plan all along. Not to take them away, but to leave them here, buried inside their own walls. She thought she'd been learning secrets she could take back to her people. Instead, she'd been building her own tomb.

The last block settled into place.

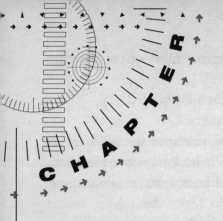

EIGHTEEN

In the utter darkness there were horrible, ear-splitting screams. Hands clutching. Nails scratching. And over it all, Sarai heard a voice screaming, pleading, "Mama! Mama!"

"Daena, I'm here!" she yelled. "I'm over here!"

She yelled again and again until she realized that she was only adding to the chaos. They were sixty people in a tiny space, blind and totally panicked. Bodies thumped against one another and against the stones. Sarai thought of shouting for silence, but she knew it would do no good.

She groped for the person next to her, felt a shoulder, and then felt a hand slapping hers away. But she didn't let go. Instead, she leaned in close and said in the calmest voice she could manage, "I am Sarai, chief of the tek clan from over the mountains. What is your name?"

"My-my name?" said a voice. "Karlo."

"Good, Karlo," she said evenly. "Now ask the person next to you his name."

"Who cares what his—"

"Just ask," she said. "It'll help."

She heard him start to ask as she turned the other direction and did the same thing. A woman answered her and followed her instructions, turning to ask the person next to her.

The affect was like a ripple passing across a pond, leaving the surface calmer than before. In answering a simple question—the simplest, most direct question, about their names—everyone in the sealed chamber calmed down, and in moments the screaming had stopped.

"Well, then," Sarai said, lifting her voice out across the dark room. "That's better."

"Mama!" Daena whimpered. "I'm over here!"

"Stay calm," Sarai said. She purposely left out her daughter's name, making the comment a reminder to everyone. "We're all in this together, and if there's a way out, we'll find it together."

"There's no way out!"

"We're trapped!"

"My leg is broken!"

"Calm." Sarai said the word again firmly. "Panic won't help anything."

"What are we going to do?" Sarai recognized Pica's voice.

"I don't know yet. But I know that I don't want to be

trampled by my own people. Thank you all for being so brave."

Sarai felt something push against her back and she wondered who had squirmed behind her when she was so tightly pressed against the wall. She went on. "Maybe the apes are only keeping us here for a while. The first thing we should do is tend to those who are injured."

She felt a jab in her spine again. "If you're not injured, try to move—easy!—toward the walls. If you're hurt, stay where you are, or try to move away from a wall to the middle—"

She stopped. Something had definitely jammed itself into her back. In the tight space, she spun around, realizing that nothing was behind her except the wall. Reaching with her hands, she felt the smooth wall suddenly broken by something sticking out. It was a piece of stone.

To her surprise, as she touched the stone, it slid out even more.

"Move back," she said. "Please, anyone who's near me, try to move away a little."

"Who are you to ask!" someone said accusingly. "We're all crammed in here—"

"It's not for me!" Sarai shot back. "One of the stones is loose!"

Space opened behind her, and Sarai inched back. The stone inched forward, and then, invisible in the darkness, it hit the ground with a dull thud, just missing Sarai's toes. Warm skin touched Sarai's hand in the darkness, fumbling, then grabbing her wrist. A moment later, Sarai heard the sound of two rocks striking, and a tiny shower of sparks flew. The room was so dark that even those tiny lights flashed brightly in her eyes, leaving ghost images. The rocks struck again, and a spark caught, hovering magically in the darkness. It grew, turning into an ember, and in that faint light she could see the outline of a torch. The ember grew into a flame, and the flame illuminated a human hand holding the torch. A face leaned close into the light where Sarai could see it.

"So I suppose you'd like to know my plan?" said Mad Luc with a grin.

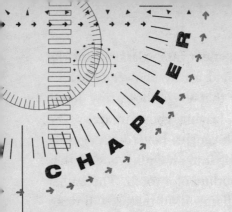

CHAPTER NINETEEN

"It was the grooves that gave me the idea," Luc explained.

His was the only face visible in the faint light of his torch, but he and Sarai knew that sixty pairs of eyes were on him.

"You know how the stone blocks are cut with those grooves. They're made so that ropes can be tied around the blocks. Then when the blocks are set into place, there's still a space for the ropes to be pulled out from underneath."

"Yeah, I had to carve lots of those grooves!" a voice called out.

"Well, I got to thinking," Luc said. "If a rope could fit in a space like that, maybe a person could, too. So I made my own space. Since the apes let us do some of our own work, I had our crew place a few stones a little out of position. I made myself a hole so that the stones wouldn't set exactly right."

"So the stone never came down right on you," Sarai said.

"Close, but no, or I'd be flatter than a fly's wing. The stone settled right down, but with about two feet of space. That's where I was."

"But how'd you get out?" Sarai asked. "Why weren't you just buried alive?"

Luc grinned. "Ah, now that's the real trick. Fixing one or two stones was no problem, but here's the thing I was really working on for the last few weeks." The torchlight moved away from Luc's face and floated down against the wall. Everyone could see the stone he'd moved, and above it, about waist high, was an opening. It penetrated deep into the wall, much farther than the firelight could reach.

"How far—?" Sarai started to ask.

"I didn't just do a couple of stones. I did a whole row."

Murmurs of surprise and approval rose up in the pitch black.

"A tunnel," Sarai said. "You designed a tunnel right under the apes' noses."

The torchlight returned to Luc's face. He was nodding and grinning. "It was pretty easy. As long as the stones were the right height, so the next layer would be even, it didn't matter what it was like underneath."

"Where does it go?"

Luc frowned. "Well, one end was supposed to lead here, when I thought this room was going to have a door. The other end leads into the temple about twenty feet down. We'll have to push a stone out there, but as long as no one's in the temple, it should be fine."

"Can we—?"

"Yes. And we should. Right now."

Sarai went first. She crawled into the hole left by the dropped stone. As soon as she was all the way in, she heard people wriggling in behind her. The tunnel was tight, but it was designed as well as every other part of the temple—straight and solid. She inched her way along, through the dark, until she reached a dead end. She listened and heard no sound—but that didn't mean much, since she was trying to listen through stone. She pushed, but it wouldn't budge.

"What's wrong?" a voice behind whispered. It was Karlo.

"There's a stone. It's stuck. I need to brace myself on something."

"What?"

"You." She planted her feet on the first solid thing she felt.

"Hey, that's my head!"

"Just keep it on your shoulders for another minute." She pushed again, now using her legs for more power. The stone groaned, then started to slide. She pushed more, and the stone slid a few more inches. Finally, it fell away from Sarai's touch, and a square of dim light appeared before her.

The stone hit the ground with a louder crash than the previous one. Sarai gritted her teeth and waited, but she heard no reaction.

"Okay," she whispered over her shoulder, "it's out. I'm going to see what's waiting for us."

Sarai wriggled out headfirst until the upper part of her body was hanging out of the wall and she felt her hands touch the ground. She pulled her feet out and stood up, looking around.

She was in the temple. Even without a roof, the temple felt enclosed and brooding, a place for hushed silence. No torches had been lit inside the unfinished building, but stars and a half moon shed faint light across the chamber. Twenty feet down one side, Sarai could see the altar, behind which lay the room that was supposed to be their tomb. There was no other sound.

Sarai was just about to turn back and tell the others it was safe when she felt an iron grip clutch the back of her leather tunic and lift her off the ground. She was turned around in midair until she was staring into the helmet-framed face of a young and fierce gorilla.

"You," the gorilla growled.

"Hello, Attar," Sarai said.

"What's wrong?" Karlo's voice called out again.

"Wait," Sarai hissed. "Just wait."

"Where did you come from?" the ape soldier asked, though he could see the tunnel as plainly as she could.

"Our paths keep crossing," she said as calmly as she

could while dangling from the gorilla's unwavering grip. "I think it's a sign."

Attar snorted. "Now you claim to read the signs of Semos. This is coincidence. An unfortunate one for you. I just came off duty and wanted to be the first to deliver a prayer to Semos in this place."

"You're quite devoted to your god."

A sneer crossed Attar's face that had nothing to do with humans. "In a few days the dome will be built, and Timon will give the first blessing. The place will be . . . spoiled, I think."

Sarai had no idea why Attar disliked the high priest, but she did know that he believed in his god. "I'm not saying I can speak for your god. But I can tell you that our paths have crossed twice now. The first time was so that I could save your life. And now, the second time . . . it seems only right, doesn't it?"

The gorilla barked out a harsh laugh. "You want me to let you go? I'm a soldier. I wouldn't be doing my duty."

"Is it a soldier's duty to kill unarmed people? Is it the will of Semos to bury people alive inside his temple?" Sarai knew she had nothing to lose. With the flexing of a single muscle, Attar could crush her. With a single cry, he could ruin any chance they had of escape. She had nothing to lose. "I don't know your god, Attar, but I can't believe he's a god who believes in such things."

Attar hesitated. His arm dipped, then raised itself, as if he were weighing her fate. "I . . . didn't know about the tomb. It didn't sit right with me, especially not in this place." His nostrils flared. He set Sarai on the ground, then leaned in so close that his flat nose nearly touched hers. "This repays our debt, human. If I hear you speak of it again, I will snap your head off before the words have left your mouth."

"Thank you," she said, exhilarated and terrified.

"Don't thank me," the gorilla said. "I am not guaranteeing your safety. You have five minutes before I raise the alarm. When those five minutes are gone, so is my debt to you."

With that, Attar shuffled over to the altar to Semos. Sarai could just make out his silhouette as he knelt before the smiling image of the ape god, his head bowed in prayer.

She leaned back into the tunnel. "Hurry!"

Sixty pairs of feet moved with the utmost quiet, muffled by pure terror. Humans with broken bones leaned on uninjured humans for support. They hurried across the temple floor, some of them glancing nervously at the figure of the ape kneeling before the altar, ignoring them.

Sarai reached the temple doors and peered outside. There were no apes in sight. With the humans supposedly entombed, there was no need for soldiery. Sarai slipped out and hurried down the wide stairs. She kept close to the wall, hurrying around to the side and eventually coming around to the back, to the wall where she and the others had worked. Here she got her bearings. Although she couldn't see it in the darkness, she knew the yellow-leafed tree lay somewhere ahead and down the hill.

As they moved, Luc hurried through the line until he

reached her. "Do you really have a plan for getting us out of the city?"

Sarai nodded. "You put a hole through an ape building. I put a hole right through their city. Come on."

She hurried forward, trusting the others to follow her, hoping they would stick close together in the darkness.

Across the flat hilltop, then down its side, was a small trail not wide enough for carts. It was probably a footpath, which served Sarai perfectly. She wound her way down the path, using only the stars and the moon for light. The path slipped between the mansions of the rich, sliding its way down the hill.

In the dark, Sarai nearly passed the yellow tree. "Psst!" A hiss stopped her, and then Ari melted out of the darkness. The female chimp looked stunned.

"You . . . did it. I mean, I'm happy for you, but how?" Ari stammered.

"We're humans," Sarai said, flashing a grin. "We're good at thinking on our feet. Now, can you show us a way out of here?"

Ari led her toward a tall white wall made of stucco—the back wall of someone's house. At the base of the wall was a large metal circle set into the ground. "This pipe carries water down the hill. There's a channel under the ground. It will meet up with bigger ones on the flats, and those will take you right beneath the wall. At the far end, somewhere out on the plains, there's an exit. It's part of the well system here."

"Will they check it?"

"No one has since I was a baby." Ari lifted away the metal cap to reveal another dark tunnel.

Sarai stopped for only a moment. "Thank you," she said. "We owe you our lives." She held out her hand. Ari took it, her long fingers wrapping around Sarai's. "Let's not speak of owing anything," the chimpanzee said. "I would help you even if I owed you nothing."

Ari looked up. The top of the temple was barely visible above the crest of the hill. "You had a hand in building that," she said. "If they had been able to kill you, Thade and Timon could have convinced themselves to forget that fact. But with you alive, it will nag at them. No matter what else they say or do, they'll never take away the fact that the temple was built by your hands."

"They'll forget, or they'll ignore it," Sarai said. "Nothing will change them." She thought of Attar. "But maybe there are others who can change."

A howl floated down to them from the hilltop, followed almost immediately by trumpets blaring an alarm. "I've got to go," Ari said. "I've gotten in enough trouble by helping. If anyone found out I did this, it could ruin my father's career. Good-bye!"

With a quickness only apes possessed, Ari sprang up to the top of the wall and dropped out of sight on the other side. Just then, Daena came up, finally able to reach her mother's side.

"Who was that?" she asked.

Sarai smiled. "Just someone who wants to help." Sarai pulled her daughter into a bear hug and squeezed. "I'm so glad you're all right," Sarai whispered. "And I'm so sorry that I've risked your life."

"I did it to myself, Mother," Daena said. "I'm the one who got caught."

"I'm the one who put you in harm's way," Sarai said. "But no more. I promise."

Daena read between the lines. "Are we going to move camp?"

Sarai nodded. "Yes. But more than that. We're bringing knowledge back with us. We helped build one building. There's no reason we can't build our own."

"Our own building?"

"No," Sarai said. She looked at Luc. "Our own city."

More horns sounded, and the humans heard shouts of alarm as ape soldiers took to the streets.

One by one the humans dropped down into the underground water channel and vanished from the eyes of the apes.

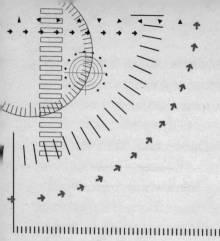

The clan, swelled to nearly a hundred, marched up the mountain slopes away from Ape City. Sarai walked at its head, with Karubi close beside her. Even now, three weeks after her return, his expressions still shifted between joy and anger. He had kept hope alive long after the rest of the clan had given her up for dead, but even his faith had been shaken. Vasich had begun to gather support for the chieftainship, and the two men had exchanged angry words.

On a day when they nearly came to blows, Sarai had walked back into camp with Daena beside her and nearly sixty humans following in her wake. Most of them did not want to return to their own clans. Those who did hoped to spread the message Sarai had delivered. Person by person, clan by clan, the word spread across the mountains and out into the plains, passing from tek to wilding: The humans would build a city on the planet of the apes.